Up Terrapin River

by

Opie Percival Read

Double 9 BOOKS

Up Terrapin River

by Opie Percival Read

ISBN: 978-93-68091-45-5

Published by

DOUBLE 9 BOOKS
2/13-B, Ansari Road
Daryaganj, New Delhi – 110002
info@double9books.com
www.double9books.com
Tel. 011-40042856

ABOUT THE AUTHOR

Opie Percival Read (1852–1939) was an American author and journalist known for his vivid portrayals of Southern life and culture. Born in Indiana, Read became well-known for his humorous and engaging storytelling, often reflecting the values, traditions, and complexities of rural communities.

His notable works include "Up Terrapin River," which captures the essence of life along a Southern river, and "A Tennessee Judge," showcasing his knack for character-driven narratives. Read's writing is characterized by rich descriptions, authentic dialogue, and a deep appreciation for the people and landscapes of the South. In addition to his novels, he contributed to various magazines and newspapers, helping to popularize Southern literature in the early 20th century. His ability to blend humor with social commentary made him a beloved figure in American literature, and his works continue to resonate with readers interested in Southern heritage and culture.

CONTENTS

CHAPTER I

Terrapin River flows through the northern part of Arkansas. It is a small stream, winding its way among hills, which here with graceful slope, and there with rugged brows, overlook the smooth and gliding water. The water, when the current is not swollen, is so clear that the stream suggests the blended flow of countless dewdrops. The brooks that flow into Terrapin River seem to float down sun-beams, gathered in the hill-tops. Up the "hollow," the cow-bell's mellow clang floats away in slowly dying echo. The spring frog struggles through a miniature forest of rank ferns; the dew that has gathered on the rugged cliffs, trickles slowly down at the rising sun's command, like tears flowing along the wrinkles of a time-worn face. The soft air plays in gentle hide-and-seek, and the wild rose, leaning over, bathes its blushing face in the mirroring stream.

The country through which Upper Terrapin River flows is slow of agricultural development. Wild hogs abound in the cane-brakes, and on the hill-sides, where the dogwood saplings tangle their blooming boughs in perfumed network, the bristling deer kills the rattlesnake, and the wild turkey-gobbler struts in barbaric vanity. The shriek of the steam-whistle has never disturbed the blue jay's noontide nap, but the water-mill, with its rhythmic splash, grinds the corn which the whistling boy, barefoot and astride the sack, brings from over the hills.

The rankest of corn grows in the "bottoms," and on the uplands the passing breezes steal the fragrance of the mellowest of horse-apples. The people, the most of them at least, are rude of speech. To them the smooth sentences of culture are as over-ripe strawberries—unfit for use. The popular estimate of a man's mental strength in this neighborhood is based upon the roughness of his expressions. There are schools, but, save in the winter, they are ill attended, for the children, so soon as they are old enough to study, are also large enough to lend important aid to the cultivation of the crops. Among those people there are many peculiar characters. They know of no country but America, and are therefore strictly American. They have a half-formed idea that there is an outside world, and that Andrew Jackson whipped it; and tradition tells them that George Washington became involved in a quarrel with a king, an awful monster with horns of gold, boxed his jaws, knocked off his horns, and sent him howling home. Their ignorance is not of the pernicious sort, but of that humorous kind which finds bright laughter clinging to the very semblance of a joke.

One afternoon a boy was plowing corn in a field not far from the river. He was apparently about sixteen years old. Under the sunburn on his face there could be seen the soft color of sadness. He was tall and well formed, and his eyes, when he looked up to tell the time of day by the sun, showed, by their wide-open earnestness—if there be anything in such surmises—that his nature was deep and his disposition frank. He had reached the end of the row, near a rail fence along whose zig-zag way there ran a road half overgrown with briers, and, after turning his horse about, was fanning himself with his broad-brim straw hat, when someone called out:

"Halloa, young man!"

The plowboy looked around and saw a man standing on the road-side, with his arms resting on the top rail of the fence. The man was of uncommon height, and his hair and bushy beard were of such fiery red as they caught a sunbeam that came down through the wavering boughs of an oak, that the boy, bursting into a laugh, cried out: "Ef you ain't on fire, I never seed er bresh heap a burnin'."

"Well," the man replied, with a smile of good nature, "I'm not exactly burning, but I am pretty warm. Drive your horse up there in the shade, and come over and sit down awhile. You look as if you are tired, and besides, I feel disposed to talk to someone."

"I am tired," the boy rejoined, "but ef my uncle wuz ter ketch me er settin' erroun', he mout norate it about that I'm lazy.

"The fresh-stirred soil shows that you have plowed many furrows to day. If your uncle should circulate such a report," he added, with another good-natured smile, "I will go with you about the neighborhood, and assist you in correcting it. Come, for I know that in talking with me, you would not be ill-spending your time."

"Then I reckon you air a school-teacher."

"No, I am nothing—nothing but an everyday sort of wayward man."

"B'l'eve I'll jine you wunst jest fur luck."

He drove his horse into a fence-corner, where the tall alder bushes cast an inviting shadow, and joined the man, who had sat down with his back against a tree.

"What is your name?" the man asked.

"John Lucas. What's yo'n?"

"Sam Potter."

"You air a mighty big man, Mr. Potter, an' I reckon you'd be a powerful fine han' ter break a yoke uv steers. Peers ter me like ef I wuz ez strong ez you air, I'd go roun' the country an' grab er-holt uv cattle, an' hold em' jest fur the fun uv seein' 'em kick." He laughed boisterously, and then, when his many shouts had ceased, Potter saw the soft color of sadness, under the sunburn on his face.

"Just now you spoke of your uncle," said Potter; "do you live with him?"

"Yes, sir. My daddy an' mammy wuz drownded a long time ergo, in the river up yander at the fo'd. Did you come that er way?"

"Yes."

"Did you see er tall rock stickin' up outen the groun'?"

"I think I did."

"Wall, I put that rock thar when I got big ernuff. It's ther tombstone."

"Are they buried there?"

"No; they wuz washed erway, an' never wuz found, an' I put that rock thar becaze it is the place whar they wuz last seed. Thar's a caterpiller on yo' neck. Let me bresh him off."

"John, I rather like you."

"Much erbleeged ter you, sir."

"And I think that there is about you excellent material for the making of a man."

"I dunno; but that's what old Alf says."

"Who is old Alf?"

"He's a nigger; but lemme tell you thar ain't no whiter man nowhar than he is. He works fur my uncle, ur ruther sorter craps it on the sheers. He don't peer to kere fur nobody much but me an' his daughter, that's all crippled up with the rheumatiz, an' when she cries in the night with her pains, it don't make no diffunce how hard he has worked durin' the day, he takes her up in his arms, an' walks erbout with her till she hushes. That's what I call a white man. Whar air you frum, Mr. Potter?"

"From almost everywhere."

"Whar do you live?"

"Nearly everywhere."

"Ain't you got nothin' ter bind you down ter one place?"

"No."

"Then you ain't ez well off ez old Alf, fur he has got that little crippled-up gal."

Potter bent upon the boy a look of contemplation, and addressing himself more than his companion, said: "Ah, young man, you do not know the force of your own philosophy. From the woods there often come the simple words of truest wisdom. Any tie of life that holds us to someone, although at times its straining may fall little short of agony, is better far than slip-shod freedom from responsibilty."

"You talk like er preacher," said the boy. "Air you one?"

"No. As I told you, I am not anything, except a tramp. I used to be a sort of lawyer, but my neglect of law texts and love for other books drove my clients away. What's that noise?"

"It's the dinner ho'n, an' I ain't sorry ter hear it, nuther. Won't you come ter the house, an' take pot-luck with us? Ain't fur. See," he added; "its right over yander on the hill."

"I will go with you, John, for to tell the truth, I am as hungry as a bear. Wait a moment until I get my carpet-bag. There is nothing in it but a shirt and a few old books—nothing in it to eat, I well know."

When they reached the stable, Potter climbed up into the loft, to throw down some corn and fodder, while John was taking the gear off of the horse.

"Now we'll go ter the house," said John, when Potter had come down, "but ez we walk erlong lemme tell you suthin'. No matter whut Aunt Liz says, don't pay no ertention to her. Mebbe she won't say nuthin' much, but ef she's on one uv her tantrums, ez Uncle Jeff calls 'em, she's mighty ap' ter make you bat yo' eyes like dust wuz er-blowin' yo' way, but keep on er battin' an' don't say nuthin'. You mout think that she is the audationist woman you ever seed, an' it mout 'pear like she's goin' ter eat you bodatiously up, but ez I said befo' keep on e' battin' an' don't say nuthin'!"

Just as they were entering the yard, a woman's shrill voice cried out: "My stairs, John, who on the top uv the yeth have you picked up this time? Wall, ef he ain't er sight fur ter see I wish I may never stir agin."

"Keep on er battin'," John whispered.

"Fur pity sake," the woman continued, "is he er red shanghai ur old Satan's whut not? John, I oughter bump yo' head ergin the wall fur pickin' up ever rag-tag an' bob-tail that comes erlong."

"Madam," said Potter, making a profound bow, "I hope I do not intrude."

"Lissen at him! My stairs, he's the biggest thing I ever seed lessen it wuz on wheels."

"Hush, an' keep on er battin'," whispered John.

"I never seed the like in my borned days," the woman went on. "The shotes got in the garden, an' momoxed up the cabbages, an' now the fetchtaked bucket had to git off down in the well. Pap, he's gone ter the blacksmith shop, an' old Alf is er-pokin' roun' summers, an' thar aint er body on the place ter do nothin'. Shew thar! The fetchtaked hens is boun' ter scratch up the red pepper, an' the red ca'f has run agin the corner uv the fence an' mighty nigh killed hisse'f. Laws er massy, it do 'pear like eve'thing is goin' ter rack and ruin."

Potter, as he stood looking at her, thought that he had never before seen so strange a creature. She was angular, and, using a country expression descriptive of extreme leanness, was rawboned. Her iron-gray hair stood out in frowsy fierceness, and her fading black eyes seemed never to have been lighted with a glow of gentleness. She had a snarling habit of wrinkling her long, sharp nose, and at times all her ill-nature would apparently find settlement on a hair-covered mole that grew on her chin.

"Madam," said Potter, "I don't think that I can repair all the damage that has been done, but if you will show me the well I will make an effort to get the bucket."

"Yander," she replied, pointing.

He went to the well, climbed down the rough stones of the wall by placing his feet on each side, and soon came up with the bucket.

"Wall, ef he ain't got it, hope I may never stir agin," the woman exclaimed. "Yander is pap."

A man well advanced in years dismounted from a swayback horse at the gate, threw a plow point on the ground and came forward. So far from being ill-looking, there was something comical about him.

"Uncle Jeff," said the boy, "this here man's name is Potter. I met him over at the fiel' an' axed him ter come ter dinner with me, an' he 'lowed he wuz as hungry as a b'ar."

"How air you, sir? Glad to make yo' 'quaintance. We ain't got no great show uv suthin' ter eat, but I reckin we kin sorter dam up yo' appetite er leetle."

"Pap," said the woman, "erbody ter hear you talk would think that we never did have nuthin' ter eat. I spize ter see er man ack like he didn't have no raisin'."

"Yas," the old fellow replied, "but I'd ruther see that than ter see er woman with the tanterums."

She cast a quick glance at him, wrinkled her nose, and then turning away, said:

"Come on in now, an' let yo vidults stop yo' mouth."

During the meal, Potter talked with the spirit of such entertainment, that at times the old man sat in open-mouth heed of his words; and the old woman, forgetful of her snappishness, bestowed upon him many glances of not unkind attention. After dinner, as they sat under the trees in the yard, the old man, addressing John, said:

"Ez it is Saturday evenin', you mout ez well knock off yo' plowin' fur the balunce uv the day. Me an' yo' aunt Liz is goin' over ter Frazier's ter stay all night, an' go frum thar ter meetin' ter-mor'. Thar's plenty ter eat cooked, an' ef yo' frien' wants ter stay here with you, all right."

The boy's face lighted up with a smile, and turning to Potter, he said:

"Wish you would stay."

"I will," replied Potter.

When old Jeff and his wife had gone, when the horses' hoofs, rattling over the flinty road, were no longer heard, John, awakening from a seeming reverie, arose, placed his hands with a sort of tender touch on the back of Potter's chair, and said:

"I am powerful glad you air goin' to stay, for you air the first great big man that ever tuck the trouble ter talk much ter me. I aint never been cuffed erroun' none, but thar is a heap er ways to make er boy feel bad without cuffin' him erroun'. Not understandin' him is er putty sho way uv hurtin' his feelin's."

"You are right, and I wonder that a boy of your surroundings should have such ripe conclusions—I mean that I am surprised at your good sense."

"I hope I don't look like er fool."

"Oh, no," Potter quickly rejoined; "there is at times about your face a glow of struggling inspiration—I mean that I like your face. If we were together very long I think I could teach you to understand my odd expressions."

"It would be ez good ez understandin' uv er book, wouldn't it?"

"Well, I could help you to understand books, and books would help you to understand me."

John sat down, and Potter, glancing at him, saw that on his face there lay a strange expression—that through the soft color of sadness a ray of hope was shining. At length the boy said:

"Uncle Jeff told me the other day that the best way fur er boy ter make er man outen hisse'f is ter git out an' hussle. He ken git ernuther boy ter plow for his vidults an' clothes. Let me go with you."

"What, do you mean that you really want to go with me?"

"Yas."

"Let me lie down under this tree and sleep a little while, John. When I awake we will talk over the matter. The fact is I have been walking all day and am very tired."

CHAPTER II

Had Potter been less tired, to sleep would not have required an effort. Nature's noises, it seemed, had conspired to "weigh the eyelids down" with pleasant drowsiness. The "chatter-jack," clinging to the nodding iron-weed's purple top, trilled his carol in praise of midsummer. The cat-bird, with soft nursing song, taught her young ones among the trumpet vines; and all the sounds were gathered up and borne away by breezes that brought sweetened scents from gullied hill-sides where larkspurs grew.

The boy sat gazing at his new-found friend, and with that innate admiration of the powerful, which is felt alike by the savage and the cultivated man, contemplated his great chest and mighty arms. Nature's sleep-wooing sounds began to affect him. He nodded, and felt himself sliding from the chair, but making no effort to regain his seat, he stretched himself upon the grass and slept.

When John opened his eyes, he saw Potter sitting on a chair looking at him.

"Well, my young friend, have you enjoyed your nap?"

"Yes, sir. Seein' you sleep so easy, made me sleepy. Now," he continued as he got up, "let's talk erbout me goin' with you."

"All right. I have just thought of a plan that will be better for us than to stroll about the country. There, I see you are disappointed. Let me explain my plan. I thought that we might rent a small farm somewhere in this neighborhood, and together cultivate it. We would not permit our work to interfere with necessary pleasure. We would not strive to make money, but would compel our farm to render us liberal support. In season we could hunt and fish, and beside our own fire-place, we could grow wise in the study of books. I would be your teacher. You spoke of the negro, old Alf. Let him and his daughter go with us. After a few years you would be fitted to go out into the world. Ah, your eyes brighten. You approve of the plan?"

"Yes, sir. If you will learn me how to read I'll go anywhar with you."

"I will take as much pains with you as if you were my son. You may wonder why I wish to settle down in such an out-of-the-way place. After awhile you shall know—I hope."

"Why do you say you hope; kain't you tell me now?"

"No, not now; perhaps never, but I hope to—well, we will talk about that some other time. All I ask of you now is to have perfect confidence in me. It is a strange request, no doubt, but you shall not regret the granting of it. Who is that coming?"

"Alf," the boy replied.

A negro, not very large, and yet seemingly possessed of much strength, climbed over the fence, hung a scythe in a tree, and approached the place where Potter and John were sitting. His face was a study of good humor, tenderness, and quaint thoughtfulness. He was more intelligent than the average man of the neighborhood. He had lived in other parts of the country, and had, before the war, belong to a North Carolina planter.

When John introduced him to Potter, and when Potter had courteously taken his hand, Alf, removing his straw hat, made a profound bow and said:

"I'se mighty pleased ter meet you, sah, caze I sees de true genermen er shinin' on yo' face; but lemme tell you, white man, I wouldn't hab you hit me wid dat fist o' yo'n fur all de co'n dars gwine ter be raised in dis yere county fur two year. Er haw, haw! If dis man doan tote er maul 'roun' wid him I neber seed one. Look here, Mr. Potter, whar you frum, nohow?"

"As I told our friend John, I am from nearly everywhere."

"Yas, sah, I better b'leve you is, better b'leve dat fur er fact, caze da ain't turnin' out sich men in dis yere 'munity at de present ercasion. Haw, haw! John, jes look at dat man, will you? Huh, er pusson would be flingin' way his time ter come projickin wid you; but lemme tell you, I likes er big man. Dar's a heep mo' comferdence ter be put in er hoss den dar is in er fox. Yas, sah, yas. How long you gwinter circle 'roun' in dis yere neighborhood, Mr. Potter?"

Potter replied by gradually unfolding his plan. Old Alf listened with his head turned to one side, like a blackbird that hears the twanging of a fiddlestring. When Potter had concluded, old Alf scratched his head for a moment, and then, addressing John, remarked:

"Dem's calkerlations, I tell you dat. Whut does yo'se'l think erbout it?"

"Fits me so well," John replied, "that I feel like gittin' out thar an' caperin' 'round like er ca'f. I ain't had no chances; Alf, you know that. I have allus been tied down here with er putty short rope, too, an' ain't had er chance ter graze out ter the end uv the line; an' I've pulled agin the rope till my neck is gettin' putty sore, yit knowin' all the time that ef I broke the rope I wouldn't know whar ter go, nor what ter do arter I got thar."

"Talkin' like er floserfer an' er gogerfy an' er rithermertik, now, chile. I thinks it will be er good thing myse'f," old Alf went on. "I knows what edycation is—knows what it is by de lack o' it. Dar's one man dat knows de full wuth o' er dollar, an' dat's de man dat ain't got it."

"You can trust me," said Potter, "to carry out with the utmost faithfulness my part of the contract. Of course, I am a stranger to both of you, but——"

"Jes hol' on er minnit," Alf broke in. "You ain't gwine tell us how hones' you is, I hope."

"Oh, no; for I do not claim to be more honest than the average man is."

"Glad ter yere you say dat, fur de man dat's allus er talkin' 'bout how hones' he is, an' sorter wants ter prove 'fo' anybody dun 'sputed it, is 'spicious o' de fack hisse'f, an' de proof is 'tended ter 'vince his own mine ez much ez it is de folks dat's listenin' ter him. Dar wuz er man in ole North Kliney dat one day while ridin' long de pike come ter er toll gate. De gate wuz open, but dar wa'nt nobody at de house. De man looked way 'cross de fiel', he did, an' he seed de toll-gate keeper at work. He pitched out ober dar, er ha'f mile through de brilin' sun, an' gin de man five cents. 'You'se de hones' man I eber seed,' said de toll-gate keeper, 'ter come all ober dis hot groun' ter gin me five cents.' 'Yas,' said de traveler, sorter drawin' his mouf down like he been eatin' er green pear, 'nobody is mo' hones' den I is.' He went on er way, an' sah, in three munts from dat time he'd dun been sent ter de penytenchy fur stealin' er hoss."

Potter laughed with good-natured uproar—laughed so loud that a bee martin, which had just alighted on the fence, flapped its wings in sudden fright and flew away.

"I am not going about making a show of honesty, Alf," said Potter, when the echo of his merriment had died in the valley.

"Glad to know dat, sah, mighty glad ter know it ef I'se gwine ter hab dealin's wid you. I ken tell de right sort o' man putty nigh ever' time. I'll go inter dis 'rangement, caze we'll hab er lot o' fun 'long wid our work."

"Do you like to fish, Alf?"

"Do er yaller dog like er fried chicken?"

"Well, I rather think he does."

"Uh, huh. Wall den, I likes ter fish."

"Do you like to hunt?"

"Do er muley steer like de sweet grass dat grows in de cornder o' de fence up ergin de bottom rail?"

"It strikes me that he does."

"Uh, huh. Wall, it strikes me dat I likes ter hunt."

"Mr. Potter," said John, "the sun is er goin' down an' its erbout time we wuz eatin' uv er snack. You an' Alf jest keep on er talkin' while I go an' put the vidults on the table."

"Dat's er monster fine boy," said Alf, when John had gone into the house. "He's sorter quiet now caze he ain't much erquainted, but airter while he'll argy er p'int wid you. Dar ain't nobody dat's got er better heart den he has, but lemme tell you, dat white boy ain't erfeerd o' ole Nick hisse'f."

"I have known him but a few hours," Potter replied, "but I have become much attached to him. Where is your daughter. Alf?"

"Ober yander in er cabin on de hillside. Ef you lissun you mout yere her singin', dat is, ef her pains ain't on her. Po' chile, she hab paid mighty dear fur de singin' she's done in dis yere life; but her reward gwine ter come airter while, Mr. Potter. Her crown goin' ter be mighty bright—rubbed bright wid de soft rag o' long sufferin', sah. Huh, my mouf waters now when I think 'bout dem huntin' sprees we'se gwine ter hab; an' lemme tell you, I knows whar de b'ars is way up de riber in de canebrakes, knows zactly whar da uses. John he's got er rifle mighty nigh long ez he is, an' I'se got one deze yere army guns—her name's Nance—dat shoots—wall, when er bullet gits outen dat gun it jes keeps on er goin', it peer like, an' I hab trained her sights down till she shoots right whar I hol's her, too. Dar, John say come on."

They went into the house. Alf did not care for anything to eat. He had eaten just before leaving home, but he found so much satisfaction in seeing his friends eat that he would take a seat near the table and watch the performance. The old negro became more and more interested in Potter, and occasionally, after a sort of digestive contemplation of a remark made by the gigantic guest, he would slowly nod his head in thorough approval. Suddenly he slapped his leg and exclaimed:

"De Lawd is already dun hepped us out on dis yere pilgumage by puttin' me in mine o' de very place we wants. Up de river 'bout six miles frum yere—John, you know de place—dar's er farm o' some sebenty-five acres, er good 'eal o' it dun cleared. Some o' it is in de riber bottom an' is monst'us rich. B'longs ter ole man Sevier dat libes 'bout two mile frum yere. Think we ken git it fur mighty low rent, fur nobody ain't lived on it fur three ur fo' year. How does dem observations strike de 'sembly?"

Potter and John were delighted with the prospect of so early a ripening of their hopes. The place was in the edge of a wild section of the country. So much the better. It was at least two miles from any other house. Better still.

"Uncle Jeff won't object to me goin'," said John, "but Aunt Liz will, not 'cause she's afeerd I won't do well, but 'cause— —"

"'Cause she's feerd you will," old Alf broke in. "Oh, I knows dat lady. Haw, haw! Knows dat lady frum way back yander way up inter de time whut ain't got yere yit, but dat doan make no diffunce. We'll whittle off all de wrinkles on de ho'n o' her ubjections."

"You are the most figurative man I ever knew," Potter smilingly remarked.

"Oh, no, sah, dat's whar you's wrong. I ain't figertive hardly none. I ken make er figer one an' ken cut er mighty caper wid er figer two, but I kain't add 'em tergedder 'cept I do it in my mine; but let us git down ter dis yere bizness. I'll go ober ter ole man Sevier's dis ebenin' an' tell him ter drap ober yere arly Monday mawnin', an' he'll come, lemme tell you, fur he is ez keen ter let us hab dat place ez we is ter git it. B'lebe I'll go dis minit," he added, taking up his hat. "Good ebenin', 'panions o' de mighty fine enterprise; good ebenin' ter you."

Potter and John talked until a late hour and then went to bed up near the clapboard roof. John soon sank to sleep. Potter lay gazing at the stars that winked through holes in the roof. A whippoorwill sat on the stack chimney and sang a lonesome song, but a cricket came out from under an old trunk, stopped in a bar of moonlight that fell on the floor, and chirruped merrily. The screech-owl, muffling and fluttering among the damp leaves of the rank greenbrier, cried with annoying cadence, but the tree-toad, with his somnolent croak, smoothed down the pillow with gentle sleepiness.

Potter was awakend by John, who called him to breakfast. Old Alf soon came. Old man Sevier would be pleased to rent his farm. He cared not so much for the money as for the improvements that might be made. The morning hours were spent in a delighted talking over of maturing plans. In the afternoon old Jeff and his wife returned. Old Jeff smiled upon the project, but the old woman wrinkled her long nose, drove to the mole on her chin the wavering lines of dissatisfaction, and declared that people who took up with every rag-tag that came along always starved to death or had to beg among the neighbors. Everyone knew that she had done her duty by John, and why he wanted to leave was something she could not understand. "You never seed this man till yistidy," the old woman went on, addressing her nephew, "an' I don't know why in the name uv common sense you wanter foller him off. Jest like men folks, anyway. Anybody ken come erlong an' lead 'em by the nose. Alf!"

"Yessum."

"Ain't you got no sense?"

"Wall'um, I'se got mo' den de man dat tried ter rive clapboards wid er razor an' den tried ter shave hisse'f wid er froe."

"I don't b'leve it."

"I kaint hep dat. Mr. Potter, doan pay no 'tention ter de lady, sah."

"You good for nuthin' black imp, you neenter be er tellin' nobody what ter do on my ercount."

"Come, come," said old Jeff; "ef you must chop wood be keerful uv yo' chips. Ef John wants ter go, w'y he's goin', that's all. He won't be so fur erway but you ken see him ever' once in er while."

"Oh, I won't be hankerin' airter seein' him. He ain't no blood kin uv mine, the Lawd knows."

"Madam," said Potter, "I am very sorry that I have caused——"

"Oh, shet ye' mouth," she snapped. "You don't know what you ase sorry uv."

With the exception of an occasional outburst from the old woman the remainder of the day was passed pleasantly. Early the next morning Sevier came over. The farm was rented on easy terms. Preparations for immediate departure were begun. John and Alf each owned a horse. Alf had two plows and several hoes. Old Jeff would lend them his wagon to haul their "plunder" over to their new home. Just as they had finished loading the wagon Alf's daughter came, walking with a crutch. She was but little more than a child, and though she bore the marks of great suffering yet she was bright and cheerful. When everything was ready, old Alf, taking hold of his daughter's arm, said: "Jule, me'n you will ride up yere on dis seat, fur I gwine ter drive. Mr. Potter, you an' John set back dar on dat straw bed."

Jeff and his wife were standing near the wagon. Mrs. Lucas, while watching the smallest detail of every movement, kept up a constant wrinkling of her nose. "This is the biggest fool caper I ever seed," she declared. "Shew, thar! the fetchtaked chickens air scratchin' up the pepper agin. The biggest fool caper I ever seed."

"I knowd o' er bigger one once," Alf replied, slily winking at Jeff.

"I don't know when it wuz."

"It wuz the time," Alf rejoined, again winking at Jeff, "that one o' the Scroggins boys clim up a sycamore tree an' tried to blow out de moon."

"Oh, go on an' keep yo' mouth shet."

"I'se gwine on, lady, but I kaint promise you ter keep my mouf shet, fur de man dat keeps his mouf shet is gwine ter starve, caze lessen he opens it he kaint put nuthen ter eat in it—er haw, haw."

"Oh, shet up. Jest ter think you would run erway and leave er half-grown crap."

"Me an' Mr. Jeff dun fixed dat, lady."

"Oh, I'll be bound he'd fix anything that don't take no trouble. Stands thar now, grinnin' like er possum. Don't peer like he'd kere whuther we raise a crap or not. Thar, drive on with you, now. Never seed sich a fool caper in my life. Bet you all starve to death."

It was so early when they drove off that the dew was still dripping from a vine-covered tree. Alf and his daughter hummed a tune. John, placing one hand on Potter's knee, looked earnestly into his face and said:

"This is the happiest day uv my life."

"Ah, my boy, we may spend many happy days together. I was just thinking how, in my case, a few hours had brought such a change—the change from a tramp to a man who is driving toward his own home."

"Whoa, whoa," exclaimed Alf, pulling on the lines. "John, reach back dar an' han' me Ole Nance (meaning his gun). Come back yere, Pete, you triflin' raskil (addressing his dog)."

"What's the matter?" Potter asked.

"Matter? Is you so blind dat you kaint see dat monst'us rattlesnake crossin' de road right up dar?"

"My gracious, what a monster!" Potter exclaimed.

"Yas," replied Alf, as he took his gun and cautiously climbed down out of the wagon, "an' he ain't eat no less'n er ha'f er dozen squirrels fur his breakfast. Git out, generman, an' watch de 'formance."

Potter and John got out. Alf continued: "Wait till he curls an' hol's up his head. Doan git up too close, caze he blow at you an' make you sick. Greshus, how pizen he is. Now hol' on."

The snake was holding up its head. Alf took deliberate aim and fired. Instantly the reptile was a twisting and tumbling mass of yellow and black and green.

"He's lookin' round fur his head," Alf remarked, "but he ain't gwine ter find it dis mawnin'. Wait till I pull off his rattles. Wants 'em ter put in my fiddle."

He pulled off the rattles while the snake was still writhing, and, as he climbed back into the wagon, remarked: "It's allus a sign o' good luck ter kill er rattlesnake dat's crossin' yo' road. Get-ep, boys."

They crossed the beautiful river and drove up the stream.

"Yander is de place," said Alf, pointing.

Yes, it was the place—a place from which John's life was to turn in a new direction—a place of learning, romance, and adventure—a place of laughter and of tears.

CHAPTER III

The house was situated on a hill near the river. From one of its windows the crystal stream could be seen. Every surrounding was attractive to a lover of nature. The house was built of logs and contained two rooms. In one of the rooms there was a great fireplace. It did not take the new occupants long to arrange their scanty collection of furniture. The girl, woman-like, regretted that no better show was made, but the men declared that the house contained everything that was strictly necessary. The third day after their arrival Potter, upon getting up from the breakfast-table (he and John ate at one large box and Alf and his daughter ate at another one of exact pattern), turned to his friends and remarked: "I am going over to Sunset to-day (a village about twenty-five miles distant), to get a Winchester rifle—saw one in a store as I came through the other day—and the books necessary for the beginning of our educational course. I have a few dollars, not many, it is true, but quite enough. John, you and Alf get as much work done as you can. Of course, the season is so far advanced that we can not get in much of a crop, but we must try to raise enough corn to run us during the winter."

Never before had John gone to work with such enjoyment. He sang as he turned over the soil. Encouragement had put a song in his mouth. Alf was delighted, and Jule was so light-hearted and so improved that she sometimes ventured out without her crutch. There was much work to be done, but they all regarded its accomplishment as a pleasure.

Potter did not return until late at night, but his friends had sat up waiting to receive him. He brought the Winchester rifle and a supply of cartridges; he brought the books, some needed dishes, a pair of shoes for John, a Sunday hat for Alf, and a calico dress for Jule.

"Oh, it's de putties thing I eber seed in my life," the girl exclaimed. "W'y dady, jes' look yere at de flowers."

"Grasshoppers, aint da?" said Alf, slyly winking at Potter.

"You know da aint. Whut you come talk dat way fur, say?" She took hold of his ears with a tender pretense of anger, and shook his head. "I'll l'arn you how ter talk dater way 'bout deze flowers. W'y da's so much like sho nuff flowers dat I ken almos' smell de 'fume. Look yere dady, we mus' git Mr. Potter suthin' ter eat."

"Aint I dun heatin' de skillet?" Alf replied. "Cose I is." He went to a box, which, nailed up against the wall, served as a "cubbard," and took out several pieces of white-looking meat.

"What sort of meat do you call that?" Potter asked.

"Dis, sah," Alf rejoined, as he began to dip the meat into a tin plate containing flour, "is some slices offen de breast o' one o' de fines' turkey gobblers I eber seed. John ken tell you how it got here."

"I wuz plowin' 'long jest before dinner," said John, "an' I hearn the gentleman gobblin' out in the woods. I wuz sorter 'stonished, too, fur it's gittin' putty late in the season fur turkeys ter be struttin' erbout. I slipped to the house an' got my rifle an' went into the woods airter him. He wuz so high up in er tree that he didn't pay no 'tention ter me, not b'lievin' I could reach him, I reckon, but I drawed a bead on his head an' down he come."

"I am glad you got him," Potter replied. "You are an excellent shot, I suppose?"

"Wall, I mout not hit er pin-head, but I reckon I could hit er steer."

"Mr. Potter," said Alf, as he stood over the fire frying the turkey breast, "wush I had axed you ter fetch de ole man some fiddle strings."

"Well, if I didn't bring you some I hope, as John's aunt would say, 'I may never stir agin.' Here they are."

"Wall, fo' greshus, ef you ain't de thoughtfules' white man I eber seed. Thankee, sah, thankee. Man mus' almos' be 'spired ter think erbout ever'thing diser way. Now, sah, we gwine ter hab some music in dis yere house. Bible say er man kaint lib by meat an' bread by itse'f; means dat folks aughter hab er little music. Ole Mars David uster play on er harp, an' I lay he done it well, too."

"The fiddle is your favorite instrument, I suppose?"

"You shoutin' now. De ho'n is er mule an' brays; de banger is er chicken dat clucks; de 'cordeon is er dog dat whines; de flute is er sheep dat blates, but de fiddle is er man dat praises de Lawd. De fiddle, sah, is de human bein' o' instrumen's. Now, set up yere ter de table, fur yo' supper's ready."

"Is that rain?" Potter remarked, as he drew his chair up to the box.

"Yas, sah, an' we'se needin' it, too. Look at John, how he's handlin' dem books. Gwine read 'em atter while, ain't you, John?"

"Yes, an' I hope befo' long, too. Ef stickin' to it counts for anything, I know I will. I'd ruther have er good education, than ter have money, an' horses, an' fine clothes."

"You shall have it, my dear boy," Potter replied. "The truest friends of this life are books. With them every man is a king; without them every man is a slave. The mind is God-given, and every good book bears the stamp of divinity. Books are the poor man's riches—the tramp's magnificent coach. I would rather live in a prison where there are books, than in a palace destitute of them."

"Dat's all mighty well, Mr. Potter," Alf interposed, "but yo' vidults gettin' cold. Books ain' gwine keep er man's supper warm. Look at John. He b'l'ebes ever' word you say, an' I doan' know but you'se right myse'f, but books ain't all. Er good heart is better den er book. Look, my little gal is settin' dar fas' ersleep, wid dat caliker coat in her arms. I mus' put her ter bed. Ah, little angel," he added, as he took her up in his arms, "you is de only book dat yo' po' daddy reads. Ter him you is de book o' dis life. All yo' leaves is got love an' tenderness writ on 'em. God bless you." He went into the other room, and closed the door.

A heavy rain fell during the remainder of the night, and at morning, as the soil was too wet to be worked, Potter suggested the advisability of a fishing expedition.

"Jule, you ain't erfeerd ter stay by yo'se'f, air you?" John asked, when all the arrangements had been made.

"Cose I ain't; an' 'sides dat, de Lawd ain't gwine let nobody hurt er po' crippled up chile ez I is."

"Your simple faith is beautiful," said Potter.

"Dar ain't no true faith, sah, dat ain't simple," Alf rejoined.

"You are right," Potter responded, "for when faith ceases to be simple, it becomes a showy pretense. Well, is everything ready?"

"Yes, sah. We'll go erbout er mile up de riber, whar dar is er good hole, an' den feesh up de stream."

The clouds had rolled away, and the day was as bright as a Christian's smile. The mocking-bird, influenced to sportive capers, flew high in the air, poured out an impulsive rhapsody, and then pretended to fall. Down the gullies, spider webs, catching the glare of the sun, shone like mirrors.

They soon reached the "hole" of which Alf had spoken, but the fish would not bite.

"I'll tell you de reason," said the old negro. "Dis water is still risin'. You kaint 'suade er feesh ter bite while de water's risin', but soon ez it 'gins ter fall, w'y da'll grab deze hooks like er chicken pickin' up co'n. Hol' him, John, hol' him. Fo' greshus, dat boy dun hung er whale. Play him roun' diser way. Doan pull him too hard, you'll break yo' line. Swing co'ners wid him; dat's right. Wait; lemme git hold de line. Yere he is. Monst'ous channel cat. Uh, whut er beauty. Weigh ten pounds ef he'll weigh er ounce."

"Good for you, John," said Potter.

"Good fur us all," replied Alf, "fur I gwine ter put dat feesh on ter cook ez soon ez I ken make er fire an' git him ready."

"It is a pity we forgot to bring a frying pan," Potter remarked.

"Doan need one, sah."

"How are you going to cook him, then?"

"You jest wait," said Alf, as he begun preparations for building a fire.

When he had made the fire, he killed the fish and dressed it.

"Are you not going to skin it?" Potter asked.

"You jest wait erwhile, now. Neber seeb sech eatin' in yo' life ez we'se gwine ter hab."

He dug some clay from a bank, poured water upon it, and begun to knead it. Then he took a piece of paper, wrapped the fish in it, and then put on a thick coating of clay.

"See; now I gwine ter put him right yere in de fire, an' let him cook erbout two hours, an' den we'll crack his shell."

They threw out their lines again, but the fish would not bite.

"It ain't no use tryin," Alf declared. "Da ain't gwine ter bite till de water ginter fall."

"Why did one of them bite?" Potter asked.

"Caze he didn' hab ernuff sense ter know dat de water want fallin', sah. You mer jest put it down fur er fack dat when er feesh bites when de water's risin', he ain't got no sense."

"We don't kere whuther they've got any sense or not, so long as they bite," John remarked.

"You're right dar; plum right. I'd ruther know dat er feesh no longer den my han' would bite, den ter know dat one ez big ez me wuz smart ernuff ter preach. Wall, ef dat boy ain't dun fotch dat book wid him."

"A good idea, John," said Potter. "We'll sit up there under that rock, and while the fish is cooking we will study our lesson."

So intent was the boy in this, his initiative step in the pursuit of knowledge, that time seemed to take the wings of the sparrow-hawk and swiftly sail away.

Alf called them to dinner. "See," said the negro, "all I had ter do wuz ter crack his shell. You axed me ef I want gwine ter skin him. See, de skin peels right off wid de paper. Openin' yo' eyes in 'stonishment, is you? Jest wait till you taste him. Set down on de rock, an' lemme he'p you ter er monst'ous piece. Sprinkle er little salt on him, dis way. Now, how do he go?"

"Best fish I ever tasted, I must say."

"Cose he is. All de flaber kep' in by dat clay."

"If we had brought our guns along, we might have had some squirrels."

"Not lessen we'd fotch de dog ter tree 'em."

"Well, we might have brought the dog."

"No, fur it's bad luck ter take er dog wid you er feeshin'. Dat's de reason I driv Ole Pete back. Tuck er dog feeshin' wid me wunst an' it want mo' den er week airter dat till I tuck de dew pizen in one o' my feet."

"Not because you took the dog, Alf, but because you went in the dew."

"Dar mout be suthin in dat fack, sah, but I know dat airterwards I went feeshin' widout takin' de dog an' soon got well o' de pizen. Tell you whut we better do airter we git done eatin'. Better go 'bout er mile up de riber ter er place whar de bass will bite like er settin' hen. De water will be fallin' by dat time. Dar's er bend in the riber right up yander, an' we ken cut off er good many steps by goin' through de bottom."

They started immediately after dinner, and had gone but a short distance into the "bottom", when old Alf stopped, took off his hat, and said:

"Dar now, dat do settle it, sho."

"What is the matter?" Potter asked.

"Doan you yere dem wolves? My greshus, whut er pack it is, too. Lissen."

"I hear them now," said Potter. "Do you hear them, John?"

"Yes, sir. I have been hearin' em fur some time, but didn't zackly know whut they was. It ain't common that they come inter this neighborhood."

"No," Alf rejoined; "an' it won't be common dat we'll go anywhar airter dis day lessen we make some mighty fast preparations. 'Tain't no use'n us tryin' ter run erway, Mr. Potter, fur da'd ketch us 'fo' we got ha'f er mile. We'll hatter climb up er tree an' wait till da goes erway. De only trouble is da mout keep us yere till we starve ter death. Da's gittin' yere. Hop up in er tree."

Potter and Alf climbed one tree; John sought refuge in another one a short distance away. The howling grew louder and louder. Alf declared that the wolves must be nearly starved or they would not cut up such "shines" in daylight. A small open space that lay between the two trees was soon alive with the howling, snarling, and snapping "varmints," as Alf termed them. Occasionally some bold leader would leap high in the air and snap at the men; others busied themselves with gnawing at the trees.

"Did'n' I tell you it wuz bad luck ter bring er dog er feeshin'?" said Alf.

"Yes," Potter replied; "but what new fact has caused you to speak of it again? The dog did not come with us, yet we have the bad luck of being treed by wolves."

"Yas, sah, yas; but if dat dog wuz yere deze wolves would eat him up, an' dat would be monst'ous bad luck fur him. How I do wush I had my gun. I wouldn' ax fur nuthin' sweeter den ter set up yere an' blow de life outen deze raskils. How you gittin' long ober dar, John?"

"Fust rate; but I'd be enjoyin' myse'f er good deal better ef I had my rifle. How I'd like ter draw er bead on that whopper; that old shaggy feller."

"Laws er massy, how I would. He's er ole pollertician, he is, an' I lay he gits ever' vote in de croud. Bet he ain't been de sheriff o' de den no less 'en er dozen times. I—whut de matter wid 'em?"

Suddenly the wolves with one impulse ceased their howling, "tucked" their tails, and ran away.

"A very gentlemanly act," Potter exclaimed. "Now we can get down from these uncomfortable perches."

"Hol' on," cried Alf. "Set right whar you is, fur dar's suthen wus den wolves round yere now. Look dar! Lawd an' de mussyful hebens proteck us!"

Two enormous panthers bounded into the open space. They cast quick glances in the direction which the wolves had taken, and then, turning about, bent their fiery gaze on Potter and the old negro. Potter turned pale, and, addressing Alf, said: "Old man, we are doomed. They will never leave us until their awful mouths are stained with our blood."

"Oh, Lawd," the old negro cried, "look down yere an' see de awful fix yo' po' servant dun got inter. Lawd, da gwine ter chaw de life outen yo' po' servant. Lawd, de bigges' one got his eyes dead set on yo' po' servant. Where'll I be dis time ter mor'. Oh, Mr. Potter, how I wush I wuz at de house drinkin' butter milk. Lawd, yo' ole servant wushes you'd strike deze pant'ers wid lightnin'. Oh, Lawd, I'd ruther die den ter be killed by er pant'er."

The panthers stood gazing at them.

Potter's pallor was gone, and on his face there rested an expression of resignation. "If they intend to do anything," said he, "I wish they would not put it off any longer. This delay is awful."

"Oh, doan say dat, Mr. Potter; oh, sweet Mr. Potter, doan say dat. Doan make no sich subjestions ter 'em, fur doan you see da's jes' waitin' fur dar mines ter git made up. My greshus, I ken feel dat monster's eyes. Da burns inter my flesh. Da ain't payin' no 'tention ter John. Look yere, dat boy ain't in de tree!"

"That's a fact," Potter cried. "What do you suppose has become of him?"

"God bless him, he's slipped down an' is gone home airter er gun. Oh, Lawd, gib de rabbit's mobement ter his legs. Let him leap ober rocks an' gullies like er fox. Dar ain't much hope fur us, though, Mr. Potter, fur by de time he gits back dem May-apple stalks down dar will be stained wid our blood. Da won't wait no longer den sundown, nohow, an' see, de sun ain't high. Ef John—mussyful hebens!"

One of the panthers had run forward, but he only sniffed the air at the root of the tree and then returned to his companion.

"Dat's right, good Lawd, hold de monster back, an' please doan let him stick his nose ergin dis tree no mo'. Look at 'em watchin' de sun. Da's sorter skittish o' de bright blaze, but when de blaze goes out an' de red glow comes, den suthen' redder will be poured on de groun'. It will be our blood. Oh, Lawd, dat raskil is lookin' harder an' harder at yo' po' servant. Wush I had er went ter er camp meetin' summers 'stead o' cumin' yere ter day, but, Lawd, it's allus de way wid er po' weak man. He's allus treadin' de path dat leads ter 'struckshun. Wush I wuz plowin' right now, eben ef de groun' is too wet. I'd ruther be anywhar—anything. Wush I wuz er 'oman er takin' in washin' fur er livin'. Wush I wuz er gal er patchin' geans britches."

"I hope John will bring my Winchester rifle," said Potter.

"He'll do dat, sah; he'll do dat."

"But do you suppose he knows how to use it?"

"Yes, sah; he's seed 'em befo'. Oh, Lawd, doan furgit whut er awful fix yo' po' servant is in. Dat sun goin' down mighty fas'. Look how da watchin' it."

It did seem as if the panthers stole an occasional and anxious glance at the sun.

"De fust pant'ers I'se seed in dis yere 'munity fur er mighty long time," old Alf went on, in his prayerful way, "an' I wushes, Lawd, dat I neber had seed deze. Wush I wuz er boy in er swimin' under some shady tree. Oh, Lawd, de raskil dun looked at de sun ergin."

He kept up a ceaseless flow of supplication. The sun seemed to sink rapidly. The shadows of the May-apple stalks were getting longer and longer. The panthers became restless. The old negro's prayer increased in earnestness. One of the panthers, the male, ran back a short distance, then coming forward with mighty bounds, sprang high in the air and caught the body of the tree.

Bang!

The panther fell to the ground. The other one ran forward, touched, with her bristly lips, her dead companion's blood, and then springing up, caught the body of the tree.

Bang!

"Thank de Lawd; thank de Lawd!" cried Alf, as he began to scramble down; "thank de Lawd."

He seized John in his arms. "Oh, de Lawd ain't gwine ter let his chillun suffer long. Yas, Mr. Potter, take holter dis young pussun. Dat's right, hug him, but look out, for you'se monst'ous strong. Bless us, de chile come back on er hoss. Sheddin' tears, too. Huh, I comin' back yere termor' an' skin deze genermen. Frien's, jes' wait er minit till I git down on my knees an' pray."

John and Potter removed their hats. The old negro sank down upon his knees, raised his clasped hands, and delivered in these words his simple prayer: "Lawd, whuteber happens un'er yo' count'nance is right, but we do thank thee fur dis ack o' hebenly mussy. Amen."

CHAPTER IV

The glare of summer was softened into the glow of autumn. In the field the dry corn-blades, gently stirring, hoarsely whispered; and the grasshopper, stiffened by the chilling dew, sat on the pumpkin where the sunlight fell. The mornings were rosy, the noontide shone with a deeper red, but the evenings came, serenely stealing, it seemed, out of the heavily-wooded land, spreading over the fields and creeping along the hill-sides where the bell-cow rang her melancholy curfew.

John was a devoted student, and Potter, almost as much interested, was never too tired to assist him. "Don't sit up too late, John," the giant would sometimes say. "To-morrow night, remember, will soon be here."

Alf, delighted to know that his violin did not disturb the cause of education, mainly spent his evenings with that instrument. One night, with sudden enthusiasm, he exclaimed:

"Look yere, Mr. Potter, I wants er little o' dat edycation merse'f. Gimme holt o' dat book er minit. Now show me er J."

"There is one," Potter replied, pointing out the letter.

"Is you sho dat's er J?"

"Yes," said Potter, smiling at John.

"No chance whuteber fur er mistake in dis yere matter?"

"None at all."

"Uh, huh. So dis yere is de J dat I'se hearn so much erbout. An' yere's er nuder one. I tell you dis yere book couldn' git er long widout de J. Whut's dis yere one?"

"That is an S," Potter replied.

"Is you sho it is er S?"

"Yes."

"Wall, wall; so yere's de S dat's been er dodgen me fur sich er long time; but I got him now."

"Here is an L," said Potter.

"I doan kere nothin' 'bout dat," Alf said, closing the book. "I wouldn' git outen de way ef I wuz ter meet er L in de road. De J an' de S wuz whut I was airter."

"Do you not want to know the other letters?"

"No, sah; I dun got ernuff. Airter wile, ef de J an S wars out, I mout call fur some more, but I'se fixed ez long ez da lasts. Jule, wouldn' you like ter know er bout de J?"

"I knows 'em all," the girl replied.

"Take ere; take ere. I neber did see so much edycation; man kaint step round yere widout trampin' on it."

"These cool days, when we have no important work to perform," said Potter, "can be well spent."

"Mine shall be," John responded. "How long will it be, you reckon, before I ken stop this sort uv splashin' with these books, an' jump right in an' swim."

"Not a great while. You must lay the worm rail, you know, before you can build the fence. In truth, you learn more rapidly than anyone else I ever knew; and sometimes, while watching your progress, I can not help but look back with pity upon the snail-like movements of my early efforts."

"Oh, dar ain't no question 'bout dat boy l'arnin'," Alf exclaimed. "Er boy dat l'arned ter break er colt ez easy ez he did one time, ain't gwine ter hab much trouble wid dis S an' J bizness. Whut, er boy dat ken slip down outen er tree widout er quick-eyed pant'er seein' him, ain't got sly mubement ernuff ter ketch deze yere books er nappin'? Doan know dat chile yit; doan know him."

One afternoon while Potter and John were at their books, and while Alf was playing on his fiddle a sort of accompaniment to a doleful tune hummed by his daughter, there came a tapping on the facing of the open door.

"Come in," Potter called.

A woman and a girl stepped into the room. John and Potter sprang up with the quick impulse of courtesy's sudden demand, and offered them seats. Alf put down his fiddle, and bowing, gave the visitors a grinning welcome.

"Where are your women folks?" the elder visitor inquired.

"We have none, madam," Potter replied, "except this girl, the daughter of this old——"

"Servant o' the Lawd," Alf interjected.

"This servant of the Lord," Potter smilingly repeated, "who assists us in tending our crop, and who is— —"

"Erbout de bes' cook in dis yere neighborhood," Alf again broke in.

"My daughter Eva and I were passing," said the woman, "and having noticed for some time that this old house was again inhabited, decided to stop and investigate. We live about five miles from here, on the Sunset road. I am Mrs. Lucy Forest, widow of Henry Forest, who died several years ago. You have heard of him, of course."

"I am a comparative stranger in this neighborhood," Potter replied.

"I ricolleck seein' him," John remarked. "Uster have something to do with the Sunday-school at Mt. Pleasant. Alf knowed him, too, I reckon."

"Lawd bless me, yas," Alf exclaimed. "I dug de man's grave."

"I remember you now," Mrs. Forest rejoined, "and I remember you, too," addressing John. "Your name," turning to Potter, "is— —"

"Excuse me for not introducing myself. My name is Potter."

"Well, I was going to say that your name was Bradshaw, and that I had seen you before."

"Excuse me a moment," said Potter, "I see your horse is loose. Let me go and hitch him for you."

"I'm younger than you, let me go," John insisted.

When John had gone, Mrs. Forest, looking after him, remarked: "That young man has a splendid face. Don't you think so, Eva?"

"Yes; strong and expressive of true refinement," the girl replied. Potter looked in admiration upon her. She was apparently but little more than fifteen years of age, but in form was well advanced toward graceful womanhood. Her eyes were large, dark, and beautiful. Her hair was as threads of fine and blackest silk, and in its graceful clustering, romance, it seemed, had found a lurking place. There was not a ruddy glow upon her cheeks, but with a creamy shading they tended toward paleness. An expression of quiet thought lay about the corners of her shapely mouth, but on her forehead, low and broad, fancy traced a brightening picture.

The girl's mother, noticing Potter's look, which had now almost deepened into a gaze, remarked: "I don't think my daughter is looking very well. For some time she has been at school over at Sunset, where there is an excellent teacher, but she studied so hard that I had to take her away."

"Mother, please don't make me out an invalid, for you know that I can walk long distances and climb steep hills without fatigue."

"Oh, I don't mean that you are an invalid, daughter; but you know yourself, Mr. Brad—Mr. Potter, that it is not well for one so young to be so devoted to books. It was her father's only trouble—I came near saying fault."

"It was his greatest pleasure," the girl suggested.

"Yes; but if it hadn't been for books he might have been a successful business man, and we might not have been compelled to leave our home in Tennessee, where I was so contented, and settle in this out-of-the-way place, and, of necessity, take up ignorance for our neighbors."

"His neighbors, the few books which he saved, are not ignorant," the girl replied. "He loved them, found them true, and left them friends to me."

"Yes, child, yes; I know all that; but it was a hardship on me, and since his death the cultivation of the farm has given me no end of trouble. Oh, I like books well enough, but unless we can write them they don't make us a living."

"But," said Potter, "they reduce a dreary and barren hour into a minute of ripe delight."

The girl clapped her hands. "I thank you for so bright a defense," she exclaimed.

"Oh, when you come ter talk erbout books," said Alf, "Mr. Potter he plum dar. Got er big luther-kivered book yere dat he read mighty nigh all de time."

"The Bible I hope," Mrs. Forest remarked.

"The Bible often, Mrs. Forest, but the book to which he refers is the Bible's wise, though sometimes sportive, child—Shakespeare."

John re-entered the room. "There's comin' up a shower," said he, "an' I took the horse to the stable."

"It is fortunate that we stopped, even though there are no women folks," Mrs. Forest replied.

Eva turned to John. "This room has somewhat the appearance of a school," she said.

"It is a school to me," John answered.

"You are anxious to learn, I suppose."

"Yes, so anxious that the time, it 'pears like, flies away befo' I l'arn anything."

"Time will seem kinder after awhile, for then you will be more able to employ it. When you want books that are full of interest, come over to our house."

Rain began to pour down. A frightened quail fluttered past the door. A baffled hawk screamed in anger. A rabbit ran into the yard and squatted under an old and tangled rose-bush. The rain ceased. The rabbit shook himself and ran away. The hawk screamed in anger.

"It is time we were going, daughter," said Mrs. Forest when a stream of sunlight came through the window. "Will you please get our horse?" she added, addressing John.

John bowed, rather awkwardly, perhaps, yet with not a bad show of courtesy, and hurried away to execute the commission.

"Mrs. Forest," said Potter, "we do not live so far apart but that we might be more neighborly in the future."

"Why, surely not," Mrs. Forest replied. "You will find everyone neighborly in this part of the country. Many of the people have nothing, you might say, except a neighborly disposition."

When the visitors were gone, and when John had again taken up his book, Potter remarked: "Excellent people, I warrant you. What do you think of that young lady, John?"

"I don't know, sir. She's so fur away frum me, it 'pears like that I can't think about her at all. Mr. Potter, do you think I'm learnin' how to talk any better than I did?"

"Yes, and very rapidly, too; but the book which you are of necessity studying now, can only serve you in a preliminary way—I mean that what you are studying now, will prepare you for grammar, and grammar will lead you into the excellencies of speech."

"Look yere," said Alf, "its erbout time I wuz er slicin' off our names, an' er puttin' 'em in de pot. I keep er tellin' you, dat edycation gittin' powerful thick round yere, but huh, when er man's hungry, he'd ruther yere suthin' er singin' in er skillet den ter fool wid er book, I doan' kere how many picters it got in it. I'll take deze yere squirl's dat we picked offen dem hickory trees dis mawnin', an' putty soon you'll yere er song in dat fryin' pan dat'll make you genermen drap dem books. I'se dun blowed my ho'n."

Early the next morning, before Potter and John had got out of bed, Alf came bustling into the room, bringing the appearance of great excitement. "Genermen," he exclaimed, "dis ain't no time ter lie yere!"

"What's the matter?" Potter demanded. "What has happened; can't you speak?"

"Cose I ken speak. Ef I couldn' speak, I couldn' tell you dat dis ain't no time ter lay yere. Whut's happened? B'ar tracks, sah; dat's whut's happened. I wus down in the fiel' jes' now ter see ef I could find any dem raskil coons t'arin' down de co'n, an' all at once I come ter er place so tangled wid stalks dat, fo' greshus, I dun thought er whirlwin' hit de co'n, but den it wuz all splained, fur dar wuz b'ar tracks mighty nigh ez big ez er ham. Huh, I dun thought somebody dun been goin' long dar er hittin' de groun' wid er maul. Let's git er bite ter eat ez soon ez we ken, an' foller de ole scounul."

Immediately after breakfast they set out to look for the bear. The tracks in the field proclaimed him to be of monstrous size. Pete, Alf's dog, well understood the importance of the pursuit. They followed the trail a long distance up the river, and then into a dense cane-brake.

"Mr. Potter, did you ever kill a bear?" John asked.

"No; the truth is I have never seen a wild one. You have killed a number of them, I suppose?"

"No, sir; but I shot one last winter, but he got away. My gun don't carry a ball large enough, I reckon, unless I mout hit him in the eye."

"Yere's de ole lady dat totes de ball," said Alf, affectionately tapping the barrel of his army gun. "Doan kere whar I hit one o' em, he gwine squeal, lemme tell you. Jes' look at ole Pete, how he prance. He uster be er mighty fine b'ar dog, but he ain't seed one in so long, dat I'se almos' afeerd dat he dun furgot how ter keep outen de way. B'ar git er holt o' er dog an' dat dog's gone, I tell you. Le's stop right yere, an' let him go on out in yander."

The dog ran forward, becoming more and more excited. The trail was evidently warm. The dog barked some distance away. "Hol' on," said the old negro. "Lissun er minut'." Another bark; followed by a distressing howl. Alf sprang forward. Potter and John followed as rapidly as they could through the tangled cane. After a tiresome struggle, they came to a small open space. There lay the dog, dead. The old negro dropped his gun, got down on his knees, and lifted the animal's bleeding head. It was some time before the old negro spoke. His companions, respecting a grief which they saw was deep and stirring, remained silent. At length old Alf said: "Po' ole frien'. Too ole an' stiff in de j'ints ter git outen de way. We's all gittin' dat way, ole frien'. We'se gittin' so ole an' stiff dat we kaint git outen de way o' trouble w'en we sees it comin' down de road. Genermen, I lubed dis yere po' dog. He didn' know nuthin' but ter lub me. He neber seed nuthin' wrong wid de ole man. No matter whut I done, it wuz all right ter him. But he gone now—I doan know whar—but he's gone. Lemme tell you, though (arising and taking up his gun), suthin' gwine suffer fur dis. Mr. Potter, you an' John go roun' dat way, an' I go dis. Ef you hear my gun, come ter me. Ef I hear yo'n, I'll come."

They separated. "I feel sorry for the old fellow," Potter remarked. "He's a man of very deep affections, with all his African peculiarities. Indeed, he has feelings finer than many a man would ascribe to one of his color."

"I know he is one of the best men I ever seed—saw," John replied. "I have hearn folks try to make out that the nigger ain't got as big a soul as the white man, but nobody's got any bigger soul than Alf has. There's his gun!"

Again they struggled through the cane, and again they came upon a small, open space. There they found Alf, sitting on a bear, smoking his pipe and fanning himself with his straw hat.

"You have him sure enough!" Potter exclaimed.

"Sah?" Alf replied, with pretended unconcern.

"I say you have killed the bear!"

"Whut b'ar?"

"Why, the one you are sitting on."

John was leaning against a tree, shaking with laughter. He understood the old man.

"Oh, dis yere b'ar."

"Yes; that bear."

"Oh, yas, sah; I got him. Tell you whut it is" (getting up, and putting on his hat), "it won't do fur er b'ar ter come killin' one o' my ole frien's. Dangerous, sah, dangerous. Wall, we'll go home now, get de hosses, an' drag dis generman ter de house."

"An enormous animal," said Potter.

"Cose he is. Oh, I ain't trampin' roun' de neighborhood er shootin' kittens, I tell you."

CHAPTER V

When the bear had been dragged home, skinned and cut up, the work of dividing with the nearest neighbors was begun. John took a choice roast over to Mrs. Forest, whose overflowing expressions of thanks quite embarrassed him, but Eva came forward with such frankness of manner that his confusion was put to instant flight.

"Come into the other room," said the girl, "and let me show you some of my books."

He followed her into a room situated at the end of a gallery that ran the full length of the old log house. The collection numbered but a few volumes, but John opened his eyes in great astonishment.

"You haven't read all these here, have you?" he asked.

"Oh, yes, some of them many times. It doesn't take long to read them all. After awhile I will lend them to you."

"I will take good care of them."

"Oh, I know that. Anyone who would not take care of a book is not worthy of the slightest trust."

Mrs. Forest came to the door. "Eva," she said, "yonder comes that good-for-nothing Bob Juckels. I wish he would stay at home. Look; he threw a stone at the calf. I could wring his good-for-nothing neck."

Eva and John went out onto the gallery. Bob Juckels climbed over the fence, though the gate was near, and, in a skulking and "scuffing" manner, approached. He was just old enough to be "gawky," and was not intelligent enough to understand even the demands of the uncouth politeness of the neighborhood. His face was covered with red freckles, his teeth protruded, and his dingy hair looked as though it might, at some time, have been chewed by a calf.

"Hi, folks," he said, as he stepped upon the gallery. "'Lowed I'd drap in an' see you erwhile. Pap wanted me ter chop sprouts outen the corners uv the fence ter-day, but I don't feel like it. Ain't this here John Lucas?"

"Yes," John replied.

"That's whut I 'lowed. I was over at ole Lucas' house one time; drapped in ter git a drink uv water, an' hanged ef that wife uv hizen didn't skeer me putty nigh ter death. I ain't been thar sense, fur it's sorter outen my range, anyhow. Eva, have you got any fresh water handy?"

"Some there in the bucket, I think," the girl replied.

"Sho it's fresh?"

"If it isn't, you know where the well is," said Mrs. Forest.

"Yas, ought ter. John, is that yo' hoss hitched out thar?"

"Yes."

"'Lowed so. Sorter looks like you—haw! haw! Say, ef you'll go my way I'll ride behind you?"

"I'm not goin' your way; but you shouldn't ride behind me if you was goin' mine."

"Reckon we'd see erbout that."

"Well, I must go," said John, addressing Mrs. Forest and Eva.

"Don't be snatched," Juckles replied.

John gave the fellow a contemptuous look; and then, after shaking hands with the ladies, and especially after listening with gratitude to their sincere declarations that he would ever be a welcome visitor at their house, mounted his horse and rode away. He had not gone far when his saddle-girth broke. He dismounted, and while he was mending it with a string, Bob Juckles climbed over a fence, and approached him.

"'Lowed I'd cut across the field an' beat you," said Bob. "That ain't much uv a nag you've got, nohow. Don't look like he could pull er settin' hen offen her nest."

"He's putty strong," John replied, "but there air some things he can't pull. He couldn't pull the truth out of you, for instance."

"Oh, you air gettin' mighty high up sense you been 'sociatin' with that ole nigger an' that big red-headed feller. I've hearn all erbout you."

"I expect you have hearn more about us than anybody cares to hear about you."

"Keep on that er way," Bob replied, "an' you'll be sharp ernuff ter drive in the ground airter while."

"Juckels, go on erway now and leave me alone. I don't like you, and I don't want to have anything to do with you."

"How do you know whuther you like me ur not, when you don't know much erbout me?"

"I know enough about you. I've seen you a number of times. Alf knows you, too."

"Alf's er ole fool."

"Go on away, now."

"Say," said Juckels, "what made you go over thar ter the wider's?"

"None of your business."

"Fine-lookin' gal they've got over thar, ain't she? Ken make er putty fair article uv pie, too, I tell you. Say, I bet I ken outrassle you fur that coat you've got on."

"I told you to go away."

"Wall, then, I ken outbox you fur that ar hat."

John had mended the girth and was trimming a switch that he had cut from a hickory sapling.

"Did you hear whut I said?" Juckels remarked.

John, without replying, was preparing to mount his horse, when Juckels took hold of his arm. John wheeled about, and with the switch gave the intruder so sharp a cut across the face that he roared with pain. "Never mind," he yelled as John rode away, "this ain't the last day in the world. You'll hear frum me one uv these days in a way that'll make you squeal."

John, upon arriving home, found his uncle and aunt. Old Jeff was wheezy with a cold which he had caught some time before, while tying fodder at night in the dew. He and his wife had met Alf, who was on his way to take them a piece of bear meat, had faced him about and compelled him to go back with them, declaring that they could take the meat home themselves.

"I never was mo' s'prized in my life than when I found you folks had suthin' ter eat over here," said Mrs. Lucas. "My consceounce alive, I wush I may never stir agin, ef I didn't 'spect ter find you all starved ter death."

Potter looked up with a broad smile, and attempted to make some sort of a pleasant reply, but had no sooner said "madam" than the old woman, using an illustration afterward employed by Alf, "fairly fluttered." "Oh don't call me er madam," she exclaimed. "Gracious knows I didn't come all the way over here ter be madamed. When a man calls a woman madam, he thinks he's done the biggest sorter day's work. Now thar's Jeff grinnin' jest like er 'possum. Do b'le've in my soul he would grin ef the woods was afire."

"I mout ef I had ter go through 'em" old Jeff replied.

"Yes, I'll be bound you would," she answered, giving, as a recognition of his reply, a sort of savage nod. "Wall, we kaint be settin' 'round here allus, Jeff. Let's be gittin' on home, fur it'll be night 'fo' we git thar, nohow."

Winter came. Snowbirds fluttered on the smoking ground where the hogs were fed. The dry and cupped leaf of the hornbeam tree floated down the shivering rivulet, carrying as a cargo the lifeless body of a cricket.

As the weather grew colder, Alf's daughter seemed to grow weaker. She spoke not of the pain she must have suffered, but all day, when the wind howled, she sat in a corner near the fire, with her wasted hands clasped and with musing gaze fixed upon the glowing coals. In the night, when the sharp sleet rattled against the window—when some homeless and abused dog howled dismally on the hill-side—old Alf would take her in his arms and walk the floor with her, whispering the while soft words of love's encouragement. The winter would soon be gone; the dry and stiffened twig would soon again be "velveted" with buds. He told her to think of the garden that he was going to clear for her in the edge of the woods.

"Doan talk erbout gittin' weaker ever' day, little angel," he would say. "W'y bless me, chile, you's gittin' heavier all time. Huh, airter while it will take er man ez strong ez Mr. Potter ter lif' you roun'." But when he would put her down and turn away from her, tears would start from his eyes. One night, after a physician had gravely shaken his head and gone away, Alf called Potter and John.

"Come in yere er minit, genermen," he said.

They followed him. A large stove had been placed in Alf's room. Two holes in the stove glared like two red eyes.

"Can we do anything for her?" Potter asked.

"I'se erfeered not; but I kaint think, sah, dat she's so much wus ter day. Yeres de genermen, Jule. You wanted me to call 'em."

She smiled in reply. Alf knelt beside the bed. "You doan feel so much wus, does you, honey?"

"No, sah; I feels much better."

"Thank de Lawd fur dat. Set down, genermen. Oh, I tole you dat doctor didn' know whut he talkin' 'bout. Is you sufferin' much pain, little gal?"

"No, sah; none er tall. Whut time is it?"

"Bout 12 o'clock."

"I thought it wuz day. Ain't dat de sun shinin' dar ergin de wall?"

"No; dat's de light frum dem holes in de stove."

"I thought de fire wuz out," she replied. "It's so col' in yere."

"Oh, no; we got er monst'us good fire. I put in some hickory chunks jes' now."

"I wush I could see de sun."

"You ken termor' mornin', honey. It's been cloudy, you know, fur two or three days, but it's cl'ar now, fur when I looked out jes' now, er thousan' stars wuz er winkin' at each uder, thinkin' dat da got er good joke on de weather."

"De moon ain't shinin', is it?" she asked.

"No. It sorter 'pears like she's got tangled up in de underbresh way over yander on de uder side de hill, but termor' mornin' de sun gwine git up early, an' fling er bushel o' gold right inter dis yere room."

"Daddy?"

"Yas, honey."

"You won't feel too bad ef I tell you suthin', will you?"

"No, darlin'."

"Daddy?"

"Yes."

"I'se dyin'."

"Oh, doan say dat." He took her hands. "My God, genermen," he exclaimed, "she is cold. Oh, fur God's sake, kain't you he'p me? John, kain't—Oh, Hebenly Father——"

"Daddy?"

"Yas, angel."

"Didn' you tell me erbout de good man dat died? Daddy, I—oh, I'se so happy—I——"

"My God, she's gone!" exclaimed the old negro; "gone, gone. Oh, God, have mercy on my po' ole heart. Genermen, leave me yere er little while."

Potter and John went out into the night. The thousand stars were still winking at each other. Without speaking the two friends turned down toward the river.

"What noise is that?" Potter asked suddenly stopping.

It was the wild wailing of Alf's fiddle. The old man was pouring out his grief.

CHAPTER VI

Three years passed. No change had come over the old house where Potter, John, and Alf lived, but the farm was no longer a place half covered with bushes and briers. It was a long time after Jule's death before old Alf regained his wonted cheerfulness; and one night when she had, for more than two years, been in her grave, old Alf got out of bed, and began to walk up and down the room. Potter, who heard him, asked if he was ill. "Oh, no, sah," he replied. "I am jes' walkin' wid de speret o' my chile."

To John there had come a great change. He had studied with unwavering determination, and had during two winters attended school at Sunset. From a charge, he had become a companion to Potter, who, during more than one conversation with Mrs. Forest and Eva, had said: "That boy has a wonderfully strong and original mind. His teacher declares that he never saw his equal. The mark he is going to make will be deeper than any furrow he has ever plowed."

Potter and John had spent many pleasant hours at the Forest house. John had read all of Eva's books. He had not stopped at this; he had bought a number of books which he found in a store at Sunset—old books, which were thought by the storekeeper to be hopelessly out of date. He had laughed when John marched proudly away with a sack full of treasures. "That feller will never make a livin'," said the storekeeper. "Why, he give me $5 for a lot of old rubbish that I've been tumblin' about the store for years." John also laughed, but with quiet joy, for in the sack there were "Burns' Poems," the "Vicar of Wakefield," "Paul and Virginia," "Plutarch's Lives," and "Macaulay's Essays." One afternoon, John and Eva were strolling along a flower-fringed road near Mrs. Forest's house, when the girl remarked:

"It is not strange to me that you are so different intellectually now from your former self. When I first saw you I knew that this time would come."

"It is so strange to me," John replied, "that I can scarcely realize it. Oh, of course, I am by no means learned, and doubtless never shall be, but every day I see the light of perseverance thrown upon mysteries which were once dark and stubborn. Eva, there is no life so wretched as that of the yearning backwoods boy. His hands are tied; the dust from the field of ignorance blinds his eyes. But there is hope for every boy. I believe that as a case of hopelessness mine was at one time without a parallel."

"Yes," she replied, "but you have sat between two remarkable teachers. On one side, a man of books, not a great philosopher, but a man of engaging fancy and bright illustration. On the other side, a child of nature—a man who can feel the pulse of a leaf, who can hear the beating of the heart of a tree."

"Yes, but those teachers came to me," John rejoined, "just as opportunities must at some time come to all boys. If I could preach to every farmer boy, or for that matter to every boy, the first word uttered should be 'books.' Yonder comes that fellow Juckels. Let us go back toward the house."

They turned back, but had not gone far when Juckels overtook them.

"Out sorter sunin' yo'selves, I see," he said. John gave him a short "Yes;" Eva said nothing.

"Tell me, they do, that you air sorter gittin' up in the picters, John."

"I am not studying pictures. I have no intention of becoming an artist."

"Oh, you know what I mean? Say, one time er good while ergo, I told you that you would hear from me in a way that would make you squeal. Ricolleck?"

"Yes, I remember."

"Wall, the reason you ain't is becaze I went off down ter my uncle's in the white oak neighborhood, an' ever' time I came back you was off at school or somewhar else. Now, don't you think it is erbout time we was havin' er settlement?"

"I don't owe you anything," John replied.

"No; but I owe you suthin'."

"All right, then, pay it."

John felt the girl's trembling touch upon his arm. He looked at her, and saw that her face had grown paler. She gave him a look of earnest meaning, and then slowly shook her head. Not another word was spoken until they were within a few steps of Eva's home. Then John, bidding her good evening, said that he must hurry on and assist Potter and Alf in feeding the cattle.

"I wish to see you a moment," said the girl, drawing him aside. "Don't have anything to do with that man." She added, in an undertone, "he is utterly without principle."

"I will keep an eye on him," John replied. "The coward ever seems to fear the light of an open eye quite as much as he does the gleaming of a weapon. Good-evening."

John walked rapidly, but Juckels, moving with a sort of dog trot, soon overtook him.

"Looks like we mout have rain, John; the sun's goin' ter bed sorter bloody, ez the feller says."

"Yes," John replied.

"Hickory switches grow putty plentiful long here, don't they?"

"Yes."

"Never wuz cut in the face with one, I reckon?"

"No."

"They say it hurts putty bad."

"You ought to know."

"Sho nuff; mebbe, then, I do."

"I should think so, if you have a good memory."

"You bet I've got er good one. Now here, I want you ter 'polyjise ter me."

"What for?"

"You know, an' you've got ter do it ur suthin' is goin' ter happen."

"Something is always happening. If something didn't happen, time would be very dull to some people."

"Yas; an' when suthin' do happen, time mout stop ter some people. You've hearn uv fellers what b'l'eves that er pistol sometimes snaps, but er knife don't, hain't you?"

"Yes."

"Wall, I'm one uv them fellers."

"There are fellows, too, that I suppose you have heard of."

"Whut sort?"

"The kind that would not hesitate a moment to knock you down and kick you across the road. I see your knife, you coward." They had stopped in the road, and were facing each other.

"Yas, an' you'll feel— —"

John knocked him down with a blow, lightning-like in its quickness, and, without waiting for him to get up, resumed his brisk walk. Juckels did not follow, but in a sort of hoarse roar exclaimed: "You'll hear from me in a way that'll make you squeal! see if you don't."

When John reached home, he found that the cattle had been fed, and that supper was waiting for him.

"Suthin' gwine ter snatch you up one deze nights an' run erway wid you," said Alf, slyly winking at Potter. "Keep on prowlin' 'round de woods at night, an' you'll see bimeby. Set up dar now an' eat some o' dem fish me an' Mr. Potter dun cotch. B'l'ebes da bites in dis airly fall weder better den da do in de spring. Yo' Aunt Liz wuz ober yere terday, an' wuz powerful 'stonished ter see dat we ain't dun starved ter death yit. When she seed deze new cheers an' table it made de ole lady open her eyes, I tell you. Seed dat pizen feller Juckels pokin' roun' down by de river 'bout dinner time. Dat feller ain't gwine ter come ter no good. I lay er rattlesnake gwine ter bite him some day. Huh, an' I lay it'll kill de snake, too."

John then related his adventure with Juckels. "Why, you ought to have stamped the life out of the scoundrel," Potter exclaimed. "Don't you know that he might hide behind a tree and shoot you. I will go over to-morrow, see his father, and tell him that unless something is done his son is likely to be badly hurt. Why, it is an outrage."

"Doan reckon it is much use ter see his daddy," Alf replied. "W'y, dat feller is older den John, an' I doan reckon his daddy ken do much wid him."

"That may be, but something must be done. By the way, this morning while strolling up the river I met two well-dressed men, horseback, who asked me if I knew who was cutting that cedar timber away up beyond Rocky Bend."

Alf opened his eyes and straightened up. "You didn' know o' co'se," he said, with the thickness of a half-strangled whisper.

"Why, yes; I told them that four or five brothers named Dun were doing it."

"Den de Lawd hab mussy on us!" the old negro exclaimed.

"What difference did it make? I don't understand you."

"Oh, I 'tended ter tell you 'bout dat, but it's too late now, for we'se gone. Lawd, da's got you po' ole servant on de hip ergin!"

"Alf, are you crazy?"

"No, sah; an' I'se erfeerd I won't be nuthin' putty soon. Mr. Potter, dat cedar timber up dar is on guberment lan', an' dem men dat axed you erbout it wuz guberment men. W'y, nobody in dis yere neighborhood would er tole on dem Duns, fur da's de wust men you eber seed. Da'll dodge dem guberment men an' come right yere airter us. Doan ax me how da'll fine out who tole on 'em, fur I lay da knows dis minit. Did anybody yere you tole 'em?"

"There was a man fishing close by."

"Dat settles it. Lawd, da dun built er nudder fire un'er yo' po' ole servant."

"I didn't think to caution Mr. Potter," said John.

"Too late ter talk erbout it now," Alf went on. "Dem Duns comin' right yere dis night, set dis house erfire an' shoot us ez we runs out."

"The situation is serious," Potter admitted.

"Serious!" Alf exclaimed. "Does you call it serious fur er man ter run outen de house ter keep frum bein' burnt up an' den git shot down like er deer? Oh, Lawd, you better take yo' po' servant home, caze he kain't git erlong down yere."

"I didn't mean to harm the Dun brothers or in the least meddle with their affairs," said Potter, "but if they hold my action to be of such mortal sin and come to this house to seek a bloody revenge I shall deem it my duty to shoot them."

"That is the way to talk," John replied.

"Yes," said Alf, "it's de way ter talk, an' it's de way ter ack, too, but de danger is in 'em settin' de house erfire. Wall, I'se got er powerful good ole gun yere, an' ef I draw down on one o' dem men he'll wish he had er staid at home, I tell you. We'd better put deze lights out, caze dem raskils ken slip up yere an' shoot us through de cracks."

Action upon the old negro's advice was immediately taken. The wind began to howl furiously. A rumbling, low and distant, proclaimed with sullen threatening the coming of a storm. Nearer, nearer the rumbling came, and glittering spears of blinding light were thrust with angry flashing through the chink holes of the wall. The wind became more violent, the rumbling burst into a deafening clap, and ragged sheets of water lashed the house. The lingering lightning, quivering in fearful dalliance, as though loth to sink back into the dark and surging cloud, wrought upon the river, which could be seen through the window, a thousand terror-breeding shapes—great monsters that lashed the water into fiery foam.

"We better put down deze yere guns an' pray erwhile," said Alf. "Oh, Lawd, is you gwine ter let de elements kill yo' po' ole servant? My greshus, yere dem limbs strikin' de house! Dar ain't been no sich er storm ez dis—mussyful hebens, is de house down! Oh, I thought we gone dat time, sho. Deze ole logs wuz put yere ter stay—dat is, I hopes so."

"This storm will protect us from the Duns until morning, at least," Potter rejoined. "This lightning will purify our air against their poisonous vapors."

"Then," said John, "let us hope that this wind is not ill. Mr. Potter, you remember the first day I ever saw you, when we were sitting in the yard discussing a plan upon which, to me at least, there has fallen such a promise of ripeness, you said that I might think it strange that you should seek to bury yourself here in the woods."

"Yes, I remember."

"And you said that some time in the future you hoped to tell me the cause."

"Yes."

"Well, is not this a most befitting time? If a storm drove you to this place let a storm drive out to me your confidence. I have often seen you put your book aside and give yourself to moments of so deep a brooding that, though I would not seek to be obtrusive, I have tried to study out your mystery. This storm, I think, is growing worse. To-morrow—well, to-morrow we may not be here. Tell me now."

A lingering, quivering light fell on Potter's face, and under the glare John could see the darkened lines of trouble.

"No, my dear boy, I can not tell you now. That I have confidence in you, you well know; that I have an affection for you, you must feel. I have watched the soft color of sadness which I once saw under the sunburn on your face grow brighter with an eager glow. I have seen your mind unfold, and each day have found something new in you to admire, but I can not tell you what you crave to know. There, the lightning is growing dimmer. From a roar the wind is shrinking to a wail."

"Yas," said Alf, "an' I thank de Lawd fur it, too; I tell you dat. It won't do ter fool wid one deze yere storms dat puts on er black nightcap an' w'ars red ribbons at its throat. I think we mout ez well lay down yere now an' sleep erwhile. Dem men ain't gwine ter come yere ter-night; but I do b'l'ebe da'll be yere in de mawnin'; an' ef da block us up in yere de neighbors will jes' let us stay yere an' starve, caze, I tell yo, da so monst'us feerd o' dem fellers."

They had not long to wait when morning came until they saw that Alf's prediction had not been an idle one; for when Potter opened the door to look out, there came a short report from an opposite hillside, and a bullet sent splinters flying from the door facing.

"Shet de do'," Alf cried. "Grab yo' guns an' lay down on de flo'. When de sun comes up da gwine shoot through deze yere cracks. Oh, Lawd, da's still atter yo' po' ole servant. Lissun how da shoot. Biz! Yere dem balls!"

"If I can get a sight at one of them," said Potter, peering through a hole in the wall, "I think that I can relieve him from duty. Boys, shoot, anyway."

A brisk firing was now begun on each side. A small mirror flew into fragments and fell on the floor. A dish pan with a ringing "tang" fell from the wall.

"Oh, de scounule," said Alf. "It's er powerful good thing for us dat dar ain't no cracks closer ter de flo'. Helloa! What's de matter? Thank de Lawd, w'y look yander; de guberment men is airter 'em."

Indeed, a deputy United States marshal and his men had arrived, and the Duns, five in number, were captured, not however until two of them had been severely wounded. The prisoners were brought to the house, where one man, a sort of physician, attended to the wounded.

"I am very sorry that we got you into trouble," said the deputy marshal, addressing Potter, "but you have greatly aided us in breaking up this gang."

"What will you do with them?" Potter asked.

"They will be sent to the United States prison at Detroit. They have stolen a great deal of valuable timber, for which the government has use, and their terms are not likely to be short. I don't think you need to fear any more trouble, as the entire gang is now broken up. Well, boys, go and get the wagon and we will haul our violent woodchoppers to Little Rock."

That night old Alf, taking down his fiddle, remarked: "Got ter hab some music, now. Oh, I tell yer dat when er man praises de Lawd wid er little music now an' den, it takes er mighty powerful evil speret ter lay his claw on him."

CHAPTER VII

One evening old Alf, having put away the supper dishes, took down his fiddle and began to twang its strings, but failing to feel his wonted interest in the instrument, put it down and then sought diversion in the humming of an old "corn-shucking" song; but again meeting with failure, he got up, sadly shook his head, and began to walk up and down the room. Potter and John, who were reading, paid no attention. Suddenly he exclaimed:

"Uh, huh, now I got it, got it sho."

"What have you got?" Potter asked.

"W'y, sah, got de reason dat I'se troubled in my mine dis ebenin'."

"Are you troubled?"

"Is I troubled? Now, dat's er fine question ter ax er man dat has been carryin' on like I has. Ain't my fiddle 'fused ter talk ter me, an' ain't er old song dun failed ter fetch de co'n-bread crumbs o' comfort? Tibby sho. Now, whut's de matter? Suthin' dat I needs. Whut is dat suthin'? W'y, I needs ter go er possum huntin', sah, dat's whut I needs. I dreamed last night dat I seed er piece o' fat meat an' er sweet pertater er raslin'. I knowed it meant suthin', but I didn' know whut till jes' now. It means dat we got ter go er possum huntin' dis yere very night, sah. How do it hit you?"

"I'm willing. What do you say, John?"

"Suits me exactly," John replied.

"Then, let us get ready and go at once," said Potter. "There is no retrospective hand that reaches so kindly out of the past and touches me with a thrill of so endearing a memory as the hand that comes out from under the hazy curtain of an Indian-summer night and gently draws me back into a hallowed past, when, with eager footsteps, I followed the negroes on my father's farm to the place where the dogs had treed."

"Yas, I reckon so," Alf replied; "I do reckon dat; yas, sah, I do. I doan know nuthin' 'bout no arm comin' out, but I knows dat de ricollection o' some frosty nights in ole North Kliny makes me wush dat I wuz dar, er boy ergin. But let us go on ef we gwine, caze it's been some time sense de oven has shined wid de sweet grease o' de possum. Deze new dogs we got, I doan know so much erbout 'em. Wush Ole Pete—neber mine, dat's all right. Lawd, yo' ole servant 'bout ter grumble ergin."

They went out into the beautiful night. Nature was so hushed that the rythmic flow of the river could be heard. The stars seemed to shine through a gauzy sheen. In the air there was a faltering promise of the coming of winter. On a log, where the moonbeams fell, there lay a substance of greenish white. It was a dead tree-toad.

"Let's cross dis fiel'," said Alf, "an' skirt 'long de edge o' de woods whar de 'simmon trees grows. Whoop—ee! [calling to the dogs]. Git 'em down, ole boys. Whoop—ee, git 'em down!"

The old negro was joyous. He hummed old tunes. "I doan know whut make dem varmints so skace ter-night," said he.

"Knowing that you were coming after them, they have doubtless all left the country," John replied.

"I reckon you's hit it, sah; I reckon you has, caze when I starts out, suthin' mighty nigh sho ter happen. Whoop—shove 'em ole boys! Whoop, push 'em!"

"Hold on a minute," said Potter, stopping. "What is the cause of that bright light over yonder?"

"Bresh heep er burnin' whar somebody cl'arin' up new groun', I reckon," Alf replied.

"Not that," John remarked. "A brush heap would hardly send its light so high."

"Dat's er fack," the old man admitted.

"That is someone's house on fire," said Potter. "Who lives over that way?"

"Miz Forest's house is ober dat way ef I ain't turned 'roun'."

"It is her house!" John exclaimed, bounding forward. "Come on!"

They ran with the speed of utmost exertion. John gained on his companions. He jumped over a rail fence without touching it. "Come on," he cried. They could now plainly see the house. The roof was in flames. No one could be seen near the burning building. "Is it possible that they are burning up?" John thought.

He reached the yard fence, cleared it at a bound, ran across the yard, sprang upon the gallery, and threw himself with all his weight against the door. It did not yield. "Eva," he cried, beating on the door. "Eva!" No answer came. He leaped from the gallery, seized the door-step, a ponderous log, staggered upon the gallery and threw the log against the door. An oak latch snapped and the door flew open. He did not rush into the room. His sense of modesty, even at such a time, forbade it, but with a loud voice he exclaimed: "For God's sake come out; your house is on fire." The next moment Mrs. Forest and Eva, almost frantic with excitement, but wrapped in the clothes which they had gathered from the bed, rushed from the room. By this time Potter and Alf had arrived. They dashed into the house to save what furniture they could. "Don't be excited," said Potter. "Fire is dropping down, but it will take quite a while for those oak rafters to burn in two. Carry out the trunks; we can save all the clothes. Here, Alf, you are too much excited. Where is John?"

John had thought of Eva's books, and although that end of the house was almost entirely wrapped in flames, was exerting himself in the dangerous work of saving the cherished volumes, and before the roof fell in, he had carried out the last book. A number of the neighbors soon arrived, for the cry of "Fire!" "Fire!" had echoed through the woods. Mrs. Forest and Eva, having dressed themselves in the barn, stood looking at the destruction of their home.

"I don't know how it could have happened," said Mrs. Forest. "It must have caught from the upper part of the chimney. I don't know how to thank you all. The fact that this is the first time I have ever been placed under such serious obligations, makes me awkward in acknowledging them. Eva, can't you say something?"

The girl stood trembling. John stood near her. "No," she replied, "I—I—don't know——" She burst into tears.

"Come, daughter, we are going home with Mrs. Patterson and stay until we can have another house built."

The next day John went over to Patterson's. Mrs. Forest and Eva, with that strong recuperative force found among people who live in the woods, had recovered from the effect of the excitement of the previous night.

"Let us walk over and look at the ruins," said John, addressing Eva.

"There is but little to look at," she replied, "but we will go."

They spoke but few words as they crossed the fields, but each one felt that the other was not unhappy. The leaves on the running brier were red, and the velvety top of the sassafras sprout was cool to the touch.

There was nothing left of the old house but a few smoldering chunks. John and Eva sat down on a log that had served as a horse-block.

"It would have been a great disappointment to me, Eva, if your books had not been saved."

"Yes," she replied, "but they were not worth so great a risk."

"Oh, the risk was nothing. All that was required was a little activity."

They were silent for some time, and then John remarked:

"How strange everything has been. I used to fear that there never would be a time when I could talk to you without embarrassment. This fear did not come from any word or action of yours, but from a true estimate of myself."

"How a true estimate?"

"Why, an almost overpowering knowledge of my own ignorance."

She gave him an imploring look. He continued:

"You have ever been kind to me. You have helped me, inspired me. I know nothing of the world, but I know gratitude. When I am reading a book, and hold so much within my grasp, the world seems very small; but when I look away at the clouds floating far beyond the hills, I then feel that the world is very large. But, Eva, may it be large or small, there is to me but one source of true happiness. You are that source, my angel. I love you—love you. When I am near you nature is more beautiful. There is religion in the soft light of your eyes. There is the thrill of deep poetry in every sound of your voice. I do not come to you with pleading, for I feel that you love me—not because I have done you a service, but because our souls, waving in a perfumed atmosphere, touch each other."

"John."

"Yes, angel."

"You are the only human being who has ever understood me; you are the only human being whom I have ever understood. Yes, I do love you—loved you when I saw you with a child's primer in your hand—loved you when I saw you a grasping student of rhetoric. That we should love each other, seems to me as natural as that the sun should shine. It could be the only result of our association."

He put his arm about her and drew her closer to him. "Eva, as you say, love could be the only result of our association; and now do you not know that there can be but one true result of our love?"

"Yes," she replied, "only one."

The neighbors soon decided to build Mrs. Forest another house. The building of a log house in the country is looked upon as a sort of holiday frolic, and there is no man in the immediate neighborhood too busy with his own affairs to lend a helping hand. The new house was built upon the same site, and after the same pattern as the old one.

Eva had, one day, just finished arranging her books, when Bob Juckels stepped upon the gallery.

"Hi," said he, as he reached into an adjoining room, drew out a chair and sat down.

"Mr. Juckels, I want you to go away from here," the girl replied.

She stood in the library door. He looked up at her, with an attempt at a smile, but with the result of an ugly grin.

"Pretty good house you got here. Woulder come over ter the raisin', but I didn't wanter meet Lucas, fur when I meet him, we're goin' ter mix. I'm me, let me tell you that." He took out a bottle of whisky, shook it, held it up, squinted at it and then took a drink. The girl was afraid of him. Her mother had gone over to a neighbor's house.

"Putty good house you've got here. Made outen green logs an' it won't burn ez easy ez the old one did. Say, did you tell Lucas that I had axed you ter marry me?"

"No; I dislike you so much that I do not mention your name to anyone."

"Good idee. Wall, I've come ter ax you agin."

"And I tell you that I wouldn't marry you to save my life. I despise you."

"That don't make no diffunce ter me, fur airter we was married erwhile you would git over that. When I axed you befo' an' you 'lowed you wouldn't, I said you would hear from me."

"Yes."

He shook the bottle again, and took another drink. "An' you did hear frum me," he said, after a few moments' silence.

"I don't know that I have."

He laughed with a low and malicious chuckle, looked about him, looked up at the rafters, looked down at the floor, chuckled again, and said:

"Ever'thing new."

"I don't understand you," Eva replied.

"Reckon not. Wimin kain't grab er p'int ez quick ez men ken. I mean that I sot yo' house afire. Hol' on, now; hol' on. Go ter cuttin' up an' it won't be good fur you, an' mo'n that, ef you ever breathe er word uv whut I've said it'll be good-by ter you an' that feller Lucas, too. Green logs mout not burn, but thar's suthin' else that will. Powder'll burn, er—haw, haw! Yes, it'll burn like er flash."

"Oh, you wretch!"

"Yas; that's whut the grasshopper 'lowed, but the wild turkey picked him up all the same. Wall, I must be shovin' erlong; sorter knockin' 'round fur my health. I'll come over agin ter-morrer an' see whut you've got ter say. But, my lady, ef you say er word ter yo' mother, ur anybody else, it'll be good-by ter the whole kit an' bilin' uv you."

A few hours later, while Potter, John, and Alf were strolling along the river bank, they came upon Juckels. He stood with one hand resting upon a rock that protruded from a rugged cliff. An empty whisky bottle lay on the ground. As the men approached, Juckels looked up with a frown, and, with thick utterance, said:

"I want you fellers ter go on erway frum here now. Never mind, Lucas, I am goin' ter settle with you."

"Any time will suit me," John replied.

"My time will suit *me*," Juckels rejoined. "It don't make no diffunce whuther it suits you or not. But I want you fellers ter go on erway frum here now, fur I got here fust an' this is mine."

"Whut is yo'n?" Alf asked.

"This possum."

"Whar's any possum?"

"Under this here rock; that's whar."

"What's er possum doin' under dat rock when dar's plenty trees fur him ter climb!" Alf asked.

"That's none uv yo' lookout," said Juckels. "He's under this rock, an' I'm goin' ter crawl up under thar arter him."

Alf looked at the ground, examined a number of tracks, and then remarked: "Co'se you ken do what you please 'bout dis yere matter, but ef you wuz er frien' o' mine I'd t'ar yo' coat mightily er holdin' ter you fo' I'd let you go up under dar."

"Yas, I reckon you would t'ar er feller's coat, an' take it erway frum him too, ef you could."

"Oh, go on up under de rock ef you wants to," Alf exclaimed; "but I tell you now dat ef you wuz er frien' o' mine I'd beg you might'ly not ter go under dar."

"You air er old thief, an' want me ter leave this possum so you ken git him."

"Come," said Potter, "there is no occasion for such language."

"This ain't none uv yo' er'fair, nuther," Juckels responded. "I'm goin' under thar, an' that's all thar is erbout it."

He threw his hat aside, kicked the whisky bottle into the river, got down on his hands and knees, and crawled under the rock. The men had turned to go away, when there issued from under the rock the most frightful noises—the yells of Juckels and the fierce shrieking of furious animals. Juckels rolled out from under the cliff. He was literally covered with wildcats. The men ran to his assistance. The animals ran back into their den. Juckels was unable to speak. He was bleeding from many wounds, and when he breathed, blood bubbled from a hole in his throat. Some time elapsed before a word was spoken.

"We must take him home," Potter said. "Cut down some saplings and we will make a stretcher."

They started on their burdensome and solemn march, and must have gone two miles, when Alf said:

"We mout ez well put him down now an' rest erwhile."

"No," replied Potter; "let us hurry on so that a physician may be summoned."

"Dar ain't no use'n er doctor," said Alf. "De man is dun dead."

So he was. They put down the stretcher. The sounds of hoofs attracted their attention.

"Yonder comes Mrs. Forest," said John.

"Yes," replied Potter, "and I will meet her and guide her away from this awful sight."

"You are the very man I want to see," cried Mrs. Forest when Potter approached within hailing distance. "I am on my way to your house to consult you," she added, reining up the horse when they met in the road. "I want to ask your advice about something. That good-for-nothing Bob Juckels has told Eva that he set fire to our house, and has declared that he will kill us all if we—I hardly know what all he didn't say, but I want to ask you if you think it best to have him arrested!"

"He is beyond the power of the law, Mrs. Forest. Yonder he lies dead."

CHAPTER VIII

Two more years, years without especial incident to the people who lived up Terrapin River, passed away. Everyone knew of John and Eva's betrothal, and as no one had any objections to offer, there came not a jar, not a harsh sound to disturb the smoothly flowing current of their affection. One evening, as Potter and John sat in the old house awaiting the return of Alf, who had gone to Sunset to make some small purchases, the young man, after many minutes of deep meditation, looked up and remarked:

"I have worked harder of late in the hope that I might make money enough to place my approaching marriage upon a sensible footing, but it seems——"

"There, my boy," Potter broke in, "there now, don't worry. Of course every man should look to the future, but not to brood in dark foreboding. We are getting along very well, and I think you may safely—there's Alf."

The old man came in bringing several bundles. "Fetchtaked fellers ober yander," said he, "put er brick under my saddle when I had my hoss hitched, an' when I got on ter come home w'y de old critter flung me in de road. Huh, when I hit de groun' I thought de whole face o' de yeth dun struck loose. Suthin' gwine obertake dem boys one deze days. Da's dun forgot erbout dem she bears dat grabbed up dem mean white chillun when da made fun o' er old servant. Suthin' gwine ter obertake 'em, I tell you. Oh, you neenter laugh, genermen, fur suthin' gwine ter slip up behin' 'em an' grab 'em, sho."

They had eaten supper, and Potter, in his favorite position, was leaning back against the wall, when a newspaper in which one of the bundles had been wrapped, attracted his attention.

"Alf, hand me that paper," said he. "I would subscribe for some paper if we lived nearer a post office. Ah! a country sheet from Kentucky. Let me see if Uncle Billie Jackson was in town yesterday, or if Aunt Nancy Phelps has the thanks of the editor for a choice lot of radishes. I see that Uncle Bob Redmond has sold a fine colt to Anthony Boyle, and here is also the startling information that Abe Stallcup has purchased the old Adams place. I suppose——" He started. The paper shook. He sprang from the chair, pressed his hands to his head, sank upon his knees, clasped his hands and exclaimed:

"Thank God! Thank God! Oh, merciful heaven, it has come at last!"

He bowed his head and wept. John and Alf stood looking on in speechless amazement.

"Thank God, it has come at last. Oh, my friends—you—you——"

"What is the matter?" John cried.

"Wait. I—I will tell you. Here," he added, "read this. Read it out for I have only seen its aim."

John took the paper and read the following:

"A number of years ago, our readers will remember, Hon. Sam Bradwell, who lived near Lexington, this State, was convicted of the murder of Colonel Joe Moore, and was sentenced to be hanged, but made his escape the night before the execution was to take place. Now comes a sequel. About two weeks ago a man named Zack Fry, supposing that he was on his death-bed, confessed that he was the murderer of Moore. But instead of dying, he soon recovered. He was then brought to trial, and, instead of attempting to make a defense, reiterated his confession. He was sentenced to be hanged, and his execution took place last Friday. The Governor has issued a proclamation declaring Bradwell innocent, and offers a reward for intelligence of his whereabouts. Bradwell was one of the most prominent men in the State. He was a bachelor and owns one of the largest and finest farms in the famous Blue Grass region. He had served three terms in the Legislature, and but for the Moore trouble would doubtless have been sent to Congress. He and Moore were not on friendly terms—in fact, they were opposed to each other in the House of Representatives, of which body Moore was also a member. Nothing has been heard of Bradwell since his escape from jail. He has no very near relatives, and his farm, we understand, is looked after by a number of his friends. There is great rejoicing, we hear, over the proof of his innocence, for he was exceedingly popular with all classes, and especially so with the more refined element. Nearly every paper throughout the country has either published or referred to the Governor's proclamation, and we sincerely trust that the wanderer may soon return home."

Potter, or Bradwell, stood complacently smiling upon John as he neared the end of the article. His excitement had passed away, leaving not the slightest trace of its sudden bursting forth. John sat in a sort of dazed silence, gazing at his friends, and Alf, whose half-open mouth bespoke a mystified state of mind, stood leaning against the wall.

"Now, my friends," said Bradwell, "you know why Sam Potter lived in this out-of-the-way place. Let us all be perfectly easy now. Alf, sit down. You look as though you were about to be hanged. I will walk up and down the room, as it would be almost impossible for me to keep still, and will tell you the story of my trouble in Kentucky. As the newspaper article states, Moore and I were members of the Legislature. One day he introduced a bill, the passage of which I did not think would be of benefit to the State. In fact, it was full of what we called buncombe, and was, I thought, intended to play upon an unthoughtful constituency and insure the re-election of its author. I opposed the measure, and was somewhat instrumental in its defeat. This inflamed Moore's anger. He denounced me in most violent terms, and swore that he would hold me to an account which might prove painful to one of us. The Legislature adjourned the next day, and, as I did not make it my business to look for Moore, I left the capital without seeing him. He lived near Lexington, to the east; I lived west. One day, several weeks later, while riding horseback to town, I saw, sitting on a fence, a hawk that had just caught a quail. I drew my pistol and fired at the hawk, but missed it. I went on into town, and, as I was going to remain but a very short time, did not put up my horse at a livery stable, but tied him to a rack in a lot in the rear of several stores. I had transacted my business, and was going through an alley leading to the lot, when I heard the report of a pistol. I hurried onward, and, upon turning into the lot, came upon the dead body of Moore. A bullet had passed through his head. Before I had recovered from the shock of so ghastly a discovery, several men ran to the place, and it was not long until a large crowd had gathered in the lot. I did not think of my position, and surely had no idea that I should be suspected. You may therefore well imagine my surprise when the sheriff arrested me. I was searched. One chamber of my revolver was empty, and, still worse, the bullet which had passed through Moore's head, and which was extracted from a cedar post, corresponded in size with the bore of my pistol. I was taken to jail. The next day bail was refused. This was annoying, but aside from being suspected of so grave a charge, I did not regard the affair as serious. I had not counted upon the men whom I had to fight. I had not thought of Moore's enraged relatives. The trial came on. There was great excitement. I had many friends, but it seemed that they were afraid of the Moores. The jury was cowed. A verdict of guilty was brought in. A motion for a new trial was overruled. My lawyers, prominent and able men, appealed to the supreme court. The decision of the court below was sustained. The date of execution was fixed. I could not realize it. One day I saw through my grated window that men were putting up a scaffold in the jail yard. My blood ran cold. Far into the night they carried their labors. Lanterns, like the red eyes of vultures, shed a lurid—I thought bloody—light upon the scene. I heard the hammers and saws. A nail glanced under the blow of a hammer and struck my window. It fell inside the cell. The hammers and saws hushed their awful noises. 'All done, Dave?' I heard someone ask. 'Yes,' came the reply; 'everything's ready.' The workmen went away. The red eyes disappeared, and all was dark. I got down from the window and found the nail. It was a large one. The window through which I had been looking was some distance from the floor. The Sheriff's officer in the yard rarely glanced at it. I heard the 'death watch' whistling in the corridor. I climbed up to the window. The ends of the bars, where they fitted into the stones on each side of the window, were made more secure with lead that had been melted and poured about them. With the nail I soon gouged away the lead from one of the bars, but the bar could not be moved. I attempted to gouge out more lead. I dropped the nail. It fell outside. In despair I seized the bar and fell backward. It broke. A thrill shot through me. Had anyone heard me? No. The 'death watch' continued to whistle. The broken bar was a powerful lever. Another bar and another one was forced out, until not one remained. I looked out. No sounds—all darkness. I went through the window, feet foremost, and dropped to the ground. Heavens, I could not scale the outer wall! I thought of the scaffold. It was near the wall. I mounted it. A rope dangled from a beam overhead. I seized the rope, swung out, turned loose and caught the top of the wall. In a moment more I was on the ground—free. I sank upon my knees and thanked God. I was afraid to go home, so, without a cent of money, I set out on my journey. I will not speak of my privations, of the weary miles I walked—of how I worked on a new railroad, and how I managed to get a few books. But I will say this, my dear boy, your face was the first to beam upon the outcast a true and generous welcome. There, there now. I am sorry that my simple recital has moved you to tears. Alf, what are you blubbering about?"

"Sorter got suthin' in dis eye jes' now, an' got suthin' in my throat, too, I b'l'ebe. Neber seed de like. Man kaint stan' erbout yere widout gittin' all used up, things flyin' roun' so."

John caught Bradwell's hand and pressed it to his breast. "My dear boy," said the giant, "your approaching marriage is now placed upon a sensible footing. You and your wife shall go with me to Kentucky. The farm is not mine, but yours and mine. The house is large, is built of stone, and in it there are many rare books. I have all the time trusted that the light of truth would fall upon that crime, and now—but we will not talk about it. John, we will go over to-morrow and tell Mrs. Forest and Eva. Alf, you shall go to Kentucky with us."

John went to bed in a whirl of happiness. He could not sleep long at a time. Joy, as well as sorrow, puts sleep to flight. Would morning never come? What can come with such slowness as a wished-for day-break? Another doze. Sunlight streamed in upon the bed.

When Bradwell had shown Mrs. Forest the newspaper article, he told his story. The ladies were much affected, and Mrs. Forest, as she wiped her eyes, said:

"Well, I called you Bradshaw, you remember. I just knew it was Brad something, for I do think that I saw you in Kentucky years ago."

Eva and John walked along the road whose edges were fringed with flowers.

"There is nothing in our way now, precious."

"No," she replied, "nothing has been in the way, nothing, dear, but your groundless concern. Our life, I know, will almost be an ideal one."

"It shall be if love and faithfulness can make it so," he replied.

They sat down on a log and talked until the horn summoned them to dinner. That afternoon, as Bradwell and John were walking toward home, the young man remarked:

"Eva has only one trouble now."

"What is that?"

"Leaving her mother."

"Is she going to leave her?"

"Of course. Are we not going to Kentucky?"

"Yes; but Mrs. Forest, or rather Mrs. Bradwell, is going with us. Oh, you young fellows don't know everything."

They shook hands and walked on in happy silence.

The day was beautiful. It was autumn, and streaks of gray could be seen in the crab-grass. Age and infirmity had given to the "chatter jack's" song a harsher sound, and the toad, avoiding the grass where the dew was chilly, stretched himself in the dusty road.

The neighbors for miles around had gathered at Mrs. Forest's house. The bashful boy in brown homespun cast a wistful eye at the dining-table, and the half-grown girl in her linsey frock longed to see the marriage ceremonies performed.

"Where is Alf?" Bradwell asked.

No one knew. Old Jeff Lucas "'lowed" that he must be prowling around looking for something to eat, and "Aunt Liz," with a violent wrinkling of her nose, declared that if he wanted anything to eat he should get it at once, for she knew he would starve to death away off there in Kentucky.

"Mandy," said Mrs. Forest, addressing a colored woman who had come to assist in waiting on the guests, "do you know where Alf is?"

"How I know whar he is?" the woman replied. "Ef he got bizness ober yere I reckon he be yere airter while."

The ceremonies were performed, and while congratulations were still being extended Alf stepped up on the gallery. "Yere," he cried, waving a piece of paper, "somebody else got tet git married yere. Come on, Mandy." He and Mandy were married. "Oh!" the old negro exclaimed, with a pretense of great surprise, "I neber did see de like o' marryin' dat's gwine on dese days. Man kaint walk roun' yere widout bumpin' ergin somebody dat's dun married."

Bradwell and Mrs. Bradwell, John and Eva, were to go to the railway station, thirty miles away, in a wagon. Alf and his wife would ride a mule. After many farewells had been exchanged, and after John had affectionately kissed his aunt, old Jeff's wife remarked:

"I jest know you air all goin' to starve ter death, but don't think I want ter keep you here, fur goodness knows I don't."

She watched the wagon until it had turned a bend in the road, and then, clasping her hands over old Jeff's shoulder, bowed her head and sobbed.

The bridal party stood on the railway platform. "Eva," said John, "are you happy?"

"Yes, my soul is filled with a quiet joy."

The train came within sight. "It is the vehicle," said John, gazing up the road, "that is to convey us to a new and happy life."

"Yes."

Bradwell lifted his hand to point out something. John seized it and pressed it to his breast.

BEHIND A BUGLER

The conversation had turned upon the war and the old soldiers' fondness for reminiscence had been freely indulged, when someone, addressing Alf Billingsly, asked if he had served during the war.

"No," Billingsly replied. "I was not in the army, but I was in one engagement. I was a boy and was living in Gallatin, Tenn., when John Morgan dashed in and captured Colonel Boon. Some time had elapsed since the Confederate forces were driven away, and the villagers, especially the boys, were almost wild with joy at the sight of gray uniform. A season of feasting followed, and then there came the report that Colonel Johnson, a dashing Federal officer, was, with a thousand picked cavalrymen, advancing upon the town. My mother gathered her children about her and took refuge in a cellar, but, feeling that my pride had been trampled upon, I escaped and mingled with the soldiers that were preparing for battle. Old wine, and whisky of less venerable age, had flowed during the feast, and many of the men and officers were drunk. Some were singing songs of more implied patriotism than of actual tune; others, with the rising fervor of tipsyness, declared that they would not go home till morning. Ah, before the next morning came many of them had gone home. I importuned a bugler to let me get on his horse behind him and ride out to the battle. He said that if I would take his canteen over to the house of a well-known old negro and bring it back full of peach brandy, I might go home with him. I did so, having left with the negro my hat and jacket as pawned evidences of good faith, and took my place behind the bugler. An officer ordered me to get down, but I begged so hard that his reckless good humor overcame his soberer sense of discipline. With shouts and songs of discordant loudness we marched out to battle. The morning was beautiful. The ironweed was in bloom, and sitting on its purple top the dryfly sang the song of midsummer. Mockingbirds flitted in the apple trees, and the bee-martin flew round and round, waiting for a sight of the honey-laden laborer that had just gone over into a field of clover. The troops dashed out upon a blue-grass plane, jeweled here and there with the rich setting of a long-cared-for and magnificent tree. Over the brow of a green slope—the phrenological bump of perception on the face of the landscape—the enemy was seen advancing. It was to be a cavalry fight. It was to be a shock of horse and a clash of sabre. I looked to the right and saw that our men were stretched out in a long line, and looking ahead, I saw that the enemy was in similar form. My friend blew his bugle. Every horse dashed forward. A line of blue dashed to meet us. I felt a keen sense of delight. My friend blew his bugle. Clash! The two lines had met with drawn sabres. It was a beautiful sight. Not a shot had been fired. There was no dust. Clash! Far to the right, as the sabres flashed, there were two long lines of brightness, broken into whirling glints of sun-ray-catching silver. I may not have had the spirit of a poet, but the beauty and not the horror impressed me. I lost not an adjunct—I failed not to catch a single shading. I saw a bee-martin catch a bee; I saw an ironweed bend its purple head beneath the touch of a lark; I saw a man, with his skull split open fall to the ground. My friend blew his bugle. The horses leaped forward. The line of blue began to grow ragged. Wild shouts arose. Gunshots with, it seemed to me, intruding noise like the yap, yap, yap of a stray dog, rang out here and there. The enemy was retreating. My friend, standing in his stirrups, waved his bugle high in the air and then blew upon it a triumphant blast. The enemy made a stand, and again the sabres flashed, but the old wine and new whisky made the Confederates impetuous. My friend blew his bugle. The opposing line broke, and then there came gunshots with, it seemed to me, a sort of revengful bark. My friend lifted his bugle, but did not blow it. I thought that he had taken pity upon the vanquished line. We bounded forward. My friend began to lean back against me. He was laughing, I could plainly see. He leaned back farther. 'Don't lean back so far,' I said. 'Stop; don't you see you are about to shove me off?' He leaned back farther. I moved to one side—reached around and took hold of the horn of the saddle. Blood spurted from the bugler's breast. I looked up and saw that death had thrown its film into his eyes. I reached down with my foot and kicked the stirrup away. The bugler leaned over and fell to the ground. I got into the saddle, rode up to a fence, threw the bridle rein over a stake, climbed down off the horse and ran away. I went back over the grassy slope. I saw a martin catch a bee; I saw the purple head of the ironweed bend beneath the touch of the lark."

IN THE CUMBERLAND MOUNTAINS

A physician told Tom Blake that he not only needed a change of scene, but that to regain his health he required absolute freedom from business cares. "I would advise you," said the doctor, "to get on a horse and ride away, no matter whither. Go to the mountains—shun the merest suggestions of civilization; in short, sleep out like a bear."

Blake attempted to act upon this advice. He stuffed a few shirts into a pair of saddlebags, mounted a jolting horse, and rode up into the grandeur of rugged mountain gorges. But to him the scenery imparted no thrill of admiration. His heart beat low, and his pulse quivered with a weakening flutter. The fox that in sudden alarm sprang across the pathway, the raccoon that, with awkward scramble, climbed a leaning tree, called not for a momentary quickening of his blood. He was passing through one of the most distressing of human trials. He had no disease; every muscle was sound. What, then, was the trouble? You shall know.

He lay at night in a bank of leaves. Now everything startled him. He trembled violently when the sun went down. Once he sprang, with a cry of alarm, from his bed of leaves. Then he lay down again, ashamed. The horse had snorted.

Farther and farther he went into the wildness of the mountains. One evening he came upon a narrow road, and, following it for some distance, saw a house. It was an old inn, with a suggestion of the brigand about it. He tied his horse to a fence made of poles and went into the house. There he found a man with a parchment face and small, evil eyes, and a woman who, on the stage, could have appropriately taken the *rôle* of hag.

"Why, come in, sir, come in," said the man, getting up and placing a chair for Blake. "Wife and I have been so lonesome for the last day or so that we have been wishing somebody would come. Haven't we, Moll?"

The woman removed a cob pipe from her mouth, drew the back of a skinny hand across her blue-looking lips, made a noise like the guttural croak of an old hen with the roup, and said, "Yes."

"You'll of course stay all night with us," the man remarked. "We can't possibly allow you to go on, especially as we are going to have falling weather. Oh, when it comes to hospitality, why, you'll find it right here. I'll go out and put up your horse."

Blake entered no objections. His deplorable condition would have forced him into a compliance with almost any sort of proposition. The man went out, put up the horse, and soon returned with a log of wood. "The more fire we have the more cheerful it will be," he explained. "Out prospecting?" he asked.

"No," Blake answered.

"Don't live nowhere near here, I reckon?"

"No."

"How long do you expect to remain in this part of the country?"

"I don't know."

The old woman mumbled and then, with a grating croak, said:

"He don't 'pear willin' ter tell much about hisse'f. Some folks is mighty curi's thater way."

"Never mind, Moll," the host quickly responded. "It ain't quite time for you to put in, except in the way of getting us a bite to eat."

She arose, without replying, and began preparations for supper.

"It is a dull time of the year with us," said the host. "It has been about two weeks since our last boarder left. But I reckon business will pearten up a little when the fishing season opens."

Blake paid no attention, except when some sharp and unexpected note in the old man's voice produced a tingling of the nerves.

Shortly after supper, Blake declared his readiness to go to bed. He was shown into a sort of shed room, separated by a thin partition from the room which he had just quitted. The old man placed a spluttering candle on the hearth, and, expressing the hope that his guest would pass a quiet and peaceful night, withdrew.

Blake lay unable to sleep. Once the spluttering candle caused him to spring up in bed. Suddenly his ears, extremely sensitive with his nervousness, caught the sounds of a whispered conversation.

"It won't do to shed blood," said the old man. "It won't do, for we made a mighty narrow escape the last time. It's impossible to get blood stains out of the house.

"I b'l'eve them saddlebags air full uv money," the hag replied.

"I don't doubt that, and we've got to have it."

"How air you goin' ter git it?"

"Poison him. I wasn't a sort of doctor all these years for nothing."

"You never was no doctor ter hurt."

"But I'll be a doctor to-night to hurt."

"How air you goin' ter pizen him? Thar ain't a speck uv pizen on the place."

"Where is that morphine?"

"Up thar in the bottle, but will that fix him?"

"Yes, and in such a way that nobody will suspect anything."

"How air you goin' ter do? Hold it under his nose?"

"Hold it under his foot!" the man contemptuously replied. "I am going to make him take it."

"How?"

"I'll fix it."

Then there occurred a whispering of which Blake caught the following:

"Think that's ernuff?" the woman asked.

"It's nearly half a teaspoonful. Enough to make five men sleep throughout eternity."

A moment later the host entered Blake's room. His manner was free from embarrassment. In one hand he held a glass containing water.

"Stranger, I don't want to disturb you, but it occurred to me just now that you looked as if you might be going to have a spell of sickness, so I thought I would bring you some medicine. I am willing to help a man, but I don't want him to be sick on my hands. I am a doctor, but I don't propose to keep a hospital."

"Suppose I refuse to take the medicine?"

"Then you'll put me to the trouble of pouring it down you, that's all. I am a mighty gentle sort of a fellow as long as everything goes on all right, but if a hitch occurs, why I am as rough as a swamp oak."

"Are you sure the medicine will not hurt me?"

"Hurt you! Why, it will do you good. Here, swallow it down."

Blake drank the contents of the glass. The host smiled, bowed, and withdrew. Then there followed another whispered conversation.

"Tuck it all right, did he?"

"Like a lamb. He'll be all right in a half-hour from now."

During fifteen or twenty minutes Blake lay quietly in bed. Then he got up, dressed himself noiselessly, arranged the bed covers to resemble the form of a man, took his saddlebags, stepped out at a back door, went to the stable, saddled his horse, mounted and rode up to a window and looked into the room which he had occupied. Cattle were tramping about the yard, and the noise made by the horse attracted no attention. He took a position so that he could, unobserved, see all that passed within the room. The "doctor" and the old woman soon entered. They made no attempt to speak in low tones.

"Whar is his saddlebags?" the woman asked.

"Under his head, I reckon. Snatch off the covers. He won't wake up."

The old woman pulled off the covers and uttered a cry of surprise. Blake tapped on the window glass.

"Say, Doc," he called, "bring me the rest of that morphine. You see, I have been a morphine eater for a number of years, but am trying to quit. Your dose came in pretty handy, for I was in a bad fix. I am all right now, and am much obliged to you. Good-night."

Less than a week from that time the "doctor" and his wife were in jail, charged with the murder of a traveler. They were hanged at Greenville last September.

A COMMERCIAL RIP-SNORTER

Several years ago I was the editor and proprietor of the New Ebeneezer *Plow Point*. It was a weekly publication, and, with its name as well as with its class of matter, appealed to the farmers, and danced a pandering jig to the shrill whistle of their prejudices. One day E. Sim Nolan, a prominent man in the community, came into my office and said:

"I have been thinking of you for the past day or two, and I think that with my keen business instincts I have unearthed the stone with which you may pave your way to fortune. Writing is a very fine accomplishment and plays its little part in journalism, but it is not the main thing. Now, the main thing in the newspaper business is to achieve success. 'How can this be done?' you naturally ask. Not by advising the county to repair the bridge over Cypress Bayou; not the editorial advising the party to organize, but by getting business. One line in a thoroughly thrifty paper is worth more and has more weight than a thousand lines in a dragging publication that has to apologize every other week for its inability to get out on time. You want a partner, not to help you write, but a commercial rip-snorter, who can run business into a corner, choke it into submission, and then drag it into the office. That's the kind of a man you need. 'Where can I find him?' you are about to ask. You have found him, or rather he has found you. I am that man. I am that commercial rip-snorter. I can go out and in two days load the *Plow Point* so full of advertisements that you'll have to put up side-boards. What do you think of it?"

"I have no doubt of your ability," I replied, "but I can not afford to pay you."

"You don't have to pay me. The work will pay for itself. Now here; say that you are making seventy-five dollars per month. Very well. The commercial rip-snorter comes in. You get one hundred and fifty dollars per month and the commercial rip-snorter gets one fifty. W'y, it's as plain and simple and guileless as the soft laughter of a child. It shall not be for one month but for all time. In short, take me in as a partner. What is the greatest business stimulant? Salary? No, sir. Proprietary interest. Give me a half interest in your paper, and it will fly higher than the kite of Franklin. It will roar louder than a cyclone, and scatter dollars where we can easily gather them up. As a rule, I am not an enthusiast. Ordinarily I am a quiet man. The soldier is quiet until his grand occasion comes."

I told him that I would think about it and give him an answer on the following day. That afternoon I consulted with several friends. The county judge declared that when Nolan put his shoulder to the wheel the wagon moved. The county attorney said that I could well afford to pay Nolan to take a half interest. That night I went to bed in a highly agreeable state of mind. The clouds were breaking away, and I could see the sun shining. The business cares of the office would be lifted off my mind, and I could devote myself to writing and to study. With nothing to do but to digest my subjects, I could write editorials that would establish me as a party leader. I dreamed of web perfecting presses, and of being consulted by great politicians. I hummed a tune before breakfast. The trade was soon consummated; and, delivering the books to Nolan, I seated myself in my inner sanctum, warmed by a stove pipe which came through from an adjoining shed occupied by a shoemaker, and gave myself up to deep thought. At last my time had come. At last the people must acknowledge my leader-writing ability. The next day Nolan brought in a few advertisements. Ah, the ripened fruit had already begun to fall.

"By the way," said Nolan, as he seated himself on a corner of my table, "I have got a great scheme on hand."

"Glad of it," I rapturously replied. "What is it?"

"A number of our most prominent men have boned me to run for sheriff."

"But will it not take up too much of your time?"

"Why, no. You see, I can be elected as easily as falling off a log, and then, as sheriff, I can flood our paper with legal advertisements."

"Nolan, you are a remarkable man."

"You just wait."

I wrote editorials in his behalf, and even left my sanctum and made speeches for him. He was elected. He turned over his newspaper books to his son, and took charge of the sheriff's office. The boy sat in the office, and, during the forenoon, whistled a circus tune. In the afternoon he got drunk. A few days after Nolan was installed, I went over to get an armful of legal advertisements. There were none on hand just at that time, Nolan told me. "In fact," said he "it has been decided not to print the delinquent-tax list this year."

I was disappointed. The boy whistled his circus tune and then went out and got drunk. The next day, when I wanted to draw five dollars, the boy gave me thirty-five cents. Bills began to come in, and my deep thought was much disturbed by them. One morning Nolan came in, and, after whistling in imitation of his son, said:

"It's pretty tough."

"What is?"

"Why, as sheriff, I've got to take charge of this office. Paper bill."

I was staggered.

"Can't we pay our bill?" I exclaimed.

"Haven't any money at present, I am sorry to say. I regret now that I ran for sheriff, for it's devilish uncomfortable to close out a partner."

I did not exactly understand it, but when he served an execution on me I went out. As sheriff, he took charge of the office, discharged his son, and took charge of the business and editorial departments. I consulted several lawyers. They said that I was out. I knew that. They didn't know how I could get in again. The law was very peculiar. I knew that, too. I found out afterward that Nolan had called on all the lawyers, and had told them that if they interfered with his affairs, he would bear down on their clients, and as most of their clients were in jail, they did not interfere. Nolan, as sheriff—and he is now serving his fourth term—is still editor and proprietor of the New Ebeneezer *Plow Point*.

HIS FRIEND FLANDERS

When the hum in the court-room had settled into an occasional whisper, the judge asked the prisoner if he would like to make a statement. The prisoner, a slender man, with hair holding a slight intention to curl, and with eyes large and willful, arose and made this statement:

John Flanders and I were the best of friends, though we were not drawn toward each other by any common ties of vocation. In the early part of my life I turned to literature, not that I expected to realize a fortune in such a pursuit, but because I could do nothing else. Flanders was a sort of general speculator. It seemed to me that every time he stepped out in the street he saw a dollar, chased it, overtook it, and put it in his pocket. My work was difficult and uncertain; and the pigeon-holes of my desk were often stuffed with rejected manuscripts. Gradually I discovered that I could not write if I knew that Flanders was in the same building in which I had a room. At first I regarded this feeling as a nervous freak, and tried to put it aside, but then, finding that every literary thought had flown away from me, I would discover that Flanders was in the building. One day when I heard his footsteps in the hall I called him into my room. "Flanders," said I, "you know that I have to make my living by literary work?"

"Yes," he replied.

"Well, but do you know that you contribute largely to my failure?"

"No," he replied; "how can that be?"

"It is in this way, Flanders: I can not write while you are in this building. Just so soon as you step into the elevator downstairs, my ideas droop and my pen splutters."

"I am sorry," he rejoined.

"I know you are," said I, "for there is not in the world a more sympathetic man than you are."

"If I am so sympathetic, then why should I disturb you so?"

"I don't know, Flanders, but you do disturb me. Now, I have a favor to ask of you."

"It shall be granted."

"It is this: please do not come into this building again."

"I will stay away," he said.

He did not come into the building again, and for a time I wrote with ease; but one day my ideas flew away and my pen cut through the paper. I knew that Flanders was not in the building, but I knew that he was in town. I strove to write, but this fact weighed upon me. I went out to look for Flanders. I found him in the Open Board of Trade, busily engaged in driving a bargain. I drew him to one side.

"Flanders," said I, "you have again put my ideas to flight."

"How so?" he asked. "I have not been in your building since you requested me to keep away."

"I know that; but you are in Chicago, and I have discovered that I can not write if we are in the same town. Now, it really makes no difference to you where you are."

"No," he replied.

"You can make a living anywhere."

"Yes."

"Well, then, leave this city."

"I will do so," said he. "I will go to New York."

I bade him an affectionate good-by, and he left on the next eastern-bound train. I returned to my work with a feeling of refreshment. My pen tripped over the paper with graceful airiness, and my thoughts, arrayed in gay apparel, sported joyously. Thus several weeks went by, but one day my pen stopped. I urged it, as a farmer urges a balky horse, but it refused to move forward. It was because Flanders was in this country. I wrote to him: "Flanders," said I, "you must leave New York—must leave the United States. I can not write if we are both under the same flag. I have a great piece of work to perform and I know that you will not seek to deprive me of the fame which its accomplishment will bring. Please leave this country."

A few days later I received the following reply: "I leave to-day for London."

Again I went to work with a thrill of pleasure. The rosebuds of thought opened with each passing breeze of inspiration. A month passed. One day my pen fell. Instantly my thoughts flew to Flanders, and I sadly shook my head. I could not write if Flanders and I lived in English-speaking countries.

I wrote to him. He was still generous, for in his reply he said: "I appreciate your feelings. To-morrow I shall sail for Asia."

Again I experienced the usual relief, and the rosebuds which had so long been covered with dust, opened with blooming freshness. Flanders wrote to me from Pekin. Then my pen fell again. I could not write if he and I were in the same world. I replied to his letter: "Flanders," said I, "come home at once."

I waited two weary months. One night, just as I had lighted my lamp and sat down to dream with De Quincy, Flanders shoved open the door and entered the room. I threw my arms about him and pressed him to me for I loved him.

"Are you glad to see me, Flanders?" I asked, shoving him into an easy seat.

"Delighted," he replied. "What is it you would have me do?"

"Nothing but sit where you are."

He looked at me with affection. His eyes were soft and glowing. I reached into my desk and took out a sharp paper-cutter, and, as Flanders was beaming upon me, I stabbed him. He sprang to his feet and threw his arms about me, but I stabbed him again and again. He sank to the floor and I sat down to my work. Oh, how my thoughts flew. With wings that were feathered with silvery down and tipped with gold, they soared higher and higher. I——

"Hold on," said the judge. "I would not have permitted this statement had I not from the first been interested in its very curiousness. You are not charged with the murder of anyone named Flanders. You found a little boy playing among the flowers in a park and slew him."

The prisoner pressed his hands to his head. "Oh," he cried, "if Flanders be not dead I can not write. He would not deprive me of the fame——"

An officer led him away.

HENDRICKS KNEW IT

Jasper Hendricks, old man Blue, Abe Stallcup, and several other men, farmers in the neighborhood, sat, one rainy day, about the fireplace in a Tennessee crossroads store. Autumn had just begun to enforce its principles—that is, a lingering mildness of atmosphere had just turned cool enough to shiver a little when the sun had sunk behind the distant timber line. The "evangelist" had made his annual fall visit to the neighborhood, and, assisted by local talent, was holding a revival in Round Pound meeting-house.

The party of men in the store had been discussing the main features of the meeting, and in their crude way had been speculating upon religion in general, when old man Blue, a deacon and an ultra-religionist, remarked:

"Wall, gentle*men*, it's all right ter talk, but when the ho'n blows, callin' us ter a final settle*ment*, w'y we jest nachully cave; that's all. The bravest man in the world would a leetle ruther stay here, ef he's in his right mind, than ter take the chances in a neighborhood (as a feller named *Hamestring* or *Hamlet*, I dunno which, once said) frum which thar ain't nobody returned ter tell us the condition uv the craps an' sich. Now I've a putty strong hope that my after-life will be smooth an' easy, but I'll jest tell you whut's er fack, I'd ruther stay here er leetle longer, even ef I hafter plow with er jumpin' coulter an' break a yoke of calves urcasion'ly, than ter go thar."

"You air right!" Stallcup responded. "At times when we air sorter shoutin' round the mourner's bench we feel like we wouldn't kere ef we wuz called erway at wunst, but airter we git out an' see the sun shine the next day, an' see the birds erhoppin' erround the straw-stack, an' lissen ter the ole jaybird that's dun picked a quarrel with the yallerhammer, w'y we feel sorter like stayin' here a while longer."

Then Jasper Hendricks spoke. Every one turned to pay him particular attention. He was the one man in the neighborhood whom no one understood. He was strikingly handsome—tall, with soft black hair that seemed to worm itself into graceful curls. He was not saintly in his deportment. Often at night, while a furious storm was raging, and while the lightning painted in frightful colors a momentary picture on the cliffs, Hendricks, half drunk and chanting a stirring tune, had been seen to gallop at desperate speed through the crash and roar of the weather's awful outbreak.

"Gentlemen," said Hendricks, "you air but pore proofs uv yo' faith. Ef you really believe whut you say you do—believe that thar is er crown that airter while will press with gentle soothin' on your troubled brows, you would long fur the time when you mout leave this world. The shinin' uv the sun an' the quarrel uv the jaybird an' yallerhammer wouldn't have no influence ter hold you back frum er everlastin' joy."

"Hendricks," said old man Blue, "you air er sort uv er poet an' kain't understan' the feelin's uv er common man."

"I'm not er poet only in feelin'," Hendricks replied, "but ef I was I'd know mo' erbout you than I do, fur the poet, erbove all others, understan's the feelin's uv the common man. It is his perfeck understan'in' uv the heart uv the common man that makes him er poet."

"Have you got any hope in the next world, Hendricks?" old man Blue asked.

"Have you?"

"Yas."

"Why?"

"Becaze, I've got er promise."

"Who made it?"

"W'y, the Lord, I think."

"Promised you that you would be perfectly happy in the next world?"

"Yas," the old man replied.

"Air you perfeckly happy in this here world?"

"No, I ain't."

"Do you believe that the Lord always keeps his promises?"

"Yas, I do."

"Then why don't you want ter go ter the next world at once? Why don't you pray fur death?"

"I don't know, Hendricks."

"I do."

"Why, then?"

"Because you don't believe the Lord has made you any promise."

"Oh, yas, I do."

"Oh, no, you don't."

"Wall, I tell you whut it is, Hendricks, no sensible man hankers airter dyin'."

"He does, if the Lord has made him a promise."

"Yas, but he wants ter wait the Lord's own time."

"A good excuse," Hendricks replied. "You want to wait the Lord's own time, an' you hope that the Lord's time will be long."

"Hendricks, you kain't blame er man for wantin' to live."

"Yes, I can, if he believes that he would be better off in another world."

"But he don't know that."

"Then he ain't got religion, an' don't b'l'eve what God says."

"Oh, yas, Hendricks. You know it would skeer you might'ly ef you knowed you had ter die ter-day."

"I'm not religious, but ter know that I had ter die ter-day wouldn't skeer me."

"I think it would, Hendricks."

"But I know it wouldn't; so now, fur the sake uv argyment, let us say that I have got ter die ter-day."

"Yas," rejoined old Blue, "we ken say it fur argyment's sake, an' it won't skeer you, but ef it was sho' 'nuff, it would."

"Wall, then, say it's sho' 'nuff."

"We ken say it, but that won't skeer you, fur you know it ain't true."

"But I know it is true."

"What, you know that you are goin' ter die ter-day?"

"Yes, sir."

"How do you know it?"

"By this fack," Hendricks replied. He drew a revolver, placed it against his head, and fired. He fell from the chair, dead. The men looked in horror upon the scene. A breeze through the open doorway stirred Hendricks' hair into beautiful curls.

WEARING OUT THE CARPET

Among the guests at a small summer hotel were a little boy and his mother. The boy's fullness of life and richness of prankish resource kept the timid, shrinking mother in a constant state of alarm; and the servants, noticing that she was afraid that her son might give offense, took pains to increase her anxiety by telling the child, in those soft but forced tones of kindness which burn worse than harshness, not to make so much noise and not to scatter bread crumbs on the steps. The proprietor's wife, an old woman whom everyone said was motherly, unconsciously took a cue from the servants, and, forgetting that her own sons and daughters were once noisy children, began to oppress the boy.

"Sh-sh—don't make a fuss," she said, meeting him in the hall. "Little boys must be seen and not heard. Go and put that ball away. You might break something. Never mind that cat. Get out of my way. I wonder what your mother can be thinking about."

"Tommie," his mother called from a neighboring room.

"Maam."

"Come here."

"I ain't doin' nothin'."

"Oh, let him alone, I pray you," said the proprietor's wife, inclining her head and smiling at the mother, who had appeared in the doorway. "I was simply afraid that he might break something with his ball, but do let him enjoy himself, I beseech you. Children will be children, you know."

"I do hope he won't cause you any trouble," the mother replied. "I do the very best I can with him, but—I—I—come here, son."

She reached out, took the boy by the hand, and drew him into the room.

"What makes you cry, mamma?"

"Because you are so bad, darling," she replied, taking him into her arms.

"I didn't know I was bad."

"But you are. You seem to make everybody miserable."

"What's miserable?"

"Unhappy."

"What's unhappy?"

"Go, sit down over there."

He climbed up on a trunk, twisted himself around, tore his clothes, got down, killed a fly on the window pane, picked up a feather which he found in a corner, threw it up and blew his breath upon it, turned over a work-basket, climbed upon the bed where his mother had lain down, put his hands on her face, gazed with mischievous tenderness into her eyes, and said:

"I love you."

She clasped him to her bosom. "You'll be a good boy, won't you?"

"Yessum, an' when that nigger makes a face at me, I won't say anything."

"Well, you must not."

"An' musn't I grab holt of the calf's tail when he shoves it through the fence?"

"No."

"Why?"

"Oh, because it will hurt him. Let mamma go to sleep now, but don't you go out."

"Nome."

The woman sank to sleep. The boy got off the bed and went to the window. He looked up at a fly that was buzzing at the top, went back to the bed, gently kissed his mother, and stole out into the hall. Exuberant with freedom, he began to gallop in imitation of a horse.

"Sh-sh!"

He was confronted by the proprietor's wife. "What are you racing around here like a mule for—say? Don't you know you are wearing out the carpet? Why don't you go somewhere and sit down and behave like a human being? Think I bought this carpet to have it scuffed out this way? Stop raking your foot on the floor that way."

He held up his hands as if, in begging for forgiveness, he would kiss her. "Don't put your greasy hands on me. Go on, now, and don't rake your feet on this carpet. I don't know what mothers these days can be thinking about."

"Tommie," his mother called.

"Yessum."

"Come here."

"Oh, I don't know what to do with you," she said, when she had drawn him into the room. "What makes you so bad?"

"I dunno; but it must be the bad man."

"Yes, and he'll get you, too, if you don't behave yourself."

"And will he hurt me?"

"Yes; he will."

"How?"

"Burn you."

"Ho! I'd shoot him."

"You couldn't."

"Why couldn't I?"

"Oh, I don't know."

"Then how do you know he would burn me?"

"Oh, I don't know that he would."

"Then what made you say that he would?"

"For gracious sake, give me a little peace."

"A little piece of bread?" he asked, while his eyes twinkled with mischief.

"Hush, sir; hush. Not another word out of you. Take your dirty hands away from my face."

"I want to hug you."

"Well, hug me, then, and sit down."

"You love me, don't you?"

"Yes, little angel," she said, pressing him to her bosom.

"More than all the houses an' railroads an' steamboats put together?"

"Yes."

To the mother the days were dragged over the field of time like the dead body of an animal. In misery lest her son should cause offense, she watched him, and, at table, hushed him. The proprietor's wife scolded him, and at last the little fellow's spirit was cowed. He crept through the hall, and, on tiptoe, to keep from wearing out the carpets, he moved through the house. He would shrink when he saw the proprietor's wife, and in his sleep he muttered apologies and declared that he would be good. One morning he awoke with a burning fever.

"I wish you would come in and see my little boy," said the mother, addressing the proprietor's wife. She went in. The little fellow looked at her, and, as a deeply-troubled expression crossed his face, said:

"I won't wear out the carpet."

"Why, no, you won't hurt the carpet. Get up and run on it all you want to."

"I can't, now."

"But you can after awhile."

Days of suffering; nights of dread. Everything had been done and the doctor had gone home. A heart-broken woman buried her face in the bedclothes. The proprietor's wife, with tears streaming down her face, stood looking upon a wasted face which had, only a short time before, beamed with mischief.

"Little boy," she said, "dear little fellow, you are going to leave us. You are going to heaven."

"No," he faintly replied, "I will be in the way, and they won't let me laugh there."

A long silence followed, and then the old woman whispered:

"He is gone."

A man with heavy boots walked on the carpet in the hall.

A BRIDEGROOM

One hot afternoon a tramp printer entered the office of the Franklin (Ky.) *Patriot*. The regular corps of compositors were sufficient to do all necessary work, but the boys were lazy and wanted to go fishing, so the tramp was given temporary employment. When the boys returned next day they were surprised, and not a little ashamed, to see that the tramp had "set up" the entire paper—work which would have taken the entire force several days to perform. When the proof-sheets were brought in, they were found to be so clean that the editor of the *Patriot* sent for the tramp.

"What is your name?" the editor asked.

"Oscar Howell."

"Where are you from?"

Mr. Howell waived his hand around in a complete circle.

"What does that mean?"

"Means that I am from everywhere."

"Do you want work?"

"That's the reason I came here."

"I mean regular work."

"Yes; but I don't want to throw anybody out of a job."

"Glad you are so honorable; but those boys out there are my sons and I am thinking of sending them to school."

"All right, then, I will take their place."

"Do you drink?"

"I wound up the ball of an extended spree the other day, but I am not going to drink any more."

"I hope your resolution may hold out."

"I will give it many a half-soling."

"Well, you may begin regular work to-morrow morning."

"All right, sir."

Within two months from that time Mr. Howell was one of the best dressed men in the town. People who had commented on his shabby appearance now called him handsome. He joined the Good Templars' lodge and mingled in the society of the tittering maidens of the village. Doctors and lawyers sought his company. He had brought a literary freshness to the town. His jokes were new; his courtesy marked. One year passed away. Mr. Howell was engaged to marry the handsomest and most intelligent young woman in the town. The girl's father and mother were delighted. Howell was envied by all the young men. The day for the wedding drew near. The "popular and enterprising tailor" had made Howell's wedding suit.

One day another tramp entered the office. Howell dropped his "make-up rule" and sprang forward to meet him.

"Why, Shorty, how are you?"

"Sorter slow," the tramp replied as he placed his elbows on the imposing-stone. "How is it with you?"

"Oh, I am flying. Going to get married to-morrow night."

"Glad to hear it. When we separated that day with a carefully divided quart, I didn't think your lines would so soon fall in such appreciative places."

"Neither did I. It is all due, though, Shorty, to my sobriety. I tell you there is no hope for the drunkard. I'll never drink any more."

"Glad. Expect to quit pretty soon myself. What sort of wedding-toggery have you got?"

"Finest you ever saw."

"Would like to see 'em. Where's your room?"

"Just across the street."

"Suppose we go over."

"All right. You ought to see my girl."

They went to Howell's room.

"By George!" exclaimed Shorty. "You will be fixed up in style, won't you?"

"I should say so. Well, it's time, for I have been a fool long enough."

"Say, put 'em on. I want to see how you will look as a bridegroom."

"I don't want to rumple 'em."

"Go ahead and put 'em on. You know that in my present plight I can't go to see you step off."

"To please you, Shorty, I'll put 'em on, but you are the only person that could cause me to yield in this matter."

He put on the clothes.

"By George, Oscar, you look like a French dancing master. Well, I'm going to take a little nip."

He took a bottle out of his pocket and shook it. "Here's some old stuff a fellow gave me at Hopkinsville. Fifteen years old. Remember the time we struck that old negro for a pint of peach brandy? Well, here's to you. Ah, hah, hah. Would you try a little?"

"No."

"Won't hurt you. Wouldn't hurt a flea. I tell you that when a fellow feels bilious a little licker is a mighty good thing for him. Ever get bilious?"

"Yes, bilious now. Haven't had any appetite for a week."

"I was 'way off the other day, but this stuff (again shaking the bottle), has set me all right."

"You don't mean to say that you have had that licker for several days?"

"Yes. Tell you what's a fact, a man doesn't want but little of this stuff, and the beauty of it is, it keeps him from drinking bad licker."

"Let me smell of it."

Howell held the bottle to his nose. Then, with a sudden impulse, his lips closed over the neck. "Ah, that is good. What sort of a time have you had since I saw you last?"

"Tough, I tell you. Take another pull and hand it over here. Recollect that song old Patsy Bolivar used to sing—'When this old coat was new?'"

"Yes," Howell replied, "I was thinking about it the other night. Let me taste your ware, as Simple Simon remarked. Getting pretty low, too."

"Yes, too low."

"That isn't bad. Say, can you sing Patsy's song?"

"Might if I had licker enough."

"Let's slip down the back stairs into that saloon."

"All right, but ain't you going to take off your wedding clothes?"

"No; we won't be down there but a few minutes."

The next day a battered bridegroom and a ragged tramp awoke in a cattle car, seventy-five miles from Franklin.

"Say, Oscar!"

"Well."

"Give me your vest. You ain't got no use for so much toggery."

"All right, here she is."

"Where shall we strike for?"

"Reckon we'd better get off at the junction and strike out down the Memphis road."

DAVE SUMMERS

HIS OWN STORY OF A ROMANCE AND ITS ENDING.

Dar ain't no frolic in whut I'm gwine ter tell. I know dat some folks thinks dat er nigger's life is made up o' laziniss an skylarkin', but dat belief, 'specially in my case, ain't de trúf. Oh, I had my fun w'en I wuz er youngster. Bless you, dar wa'n't er pusson in de neighborhood dat hankered atter mischief mo' den Dave Summers did, but 'stead o' ole age bringin' dat peace an' rest, which, eben in de libely time o' youth, sensible pussons looks forward ter, dar come trouble o' de blackest sort.

W'en I wuz erbout fifty years ole, de notion got inter my head dat I aughter preach. I doan know how it got dar—sholy not becaze I had been thinkin' erbout it—fur de fust thing I know'd erbout it wuz wakin' up one mawnin' wid de idee. I talked wid some o' my frien's an' da said: "Dave, dat is er call, an' you better not be projickin' wid it. De speret wants yer ter fling yer voice inter de gospul work an' you better not make er Jonah o' yerse'f by tryin' ter run erway."

"But how's I gwine ter preach?" I axed. "It's 'bout ez much ez I ken do ter read."

"De Lawd ain't axed you ter read," one o' my frien's says. "He axes yer ter preach; ef you ken read er little, you ken l'arn how ter read mo'."

I went erway, mighty troubled in my mine. My wife had been dead fur sebrel years, an' not habbin' any chillum I libed by myse'f in er cabin on er big plan'ation. I shet myse'f up an' prayed. De naixt mawnin' my load 'peared ter be heavier. Dar wa'n't nuthin' left fur me, so I says: "I will preach. I will get somebody ter l'arn me how ter read mo' an' I will preach de gospul de bes' I knows how." Den I thought o' my load, but it wuz gone. It wa'n't long till I stood up in de pulpit. Dar wuz sebrel smart men in de church, an' it 'peared ter 'muze 'em might'ly ter yere ez ignunt er man ez I wuz talk erbout heaben an' de souls o' men. Ah, Lawd! ignunce ken fling ez much light on some subjec's ez de greates' 'arthly wisdom ken. I went at my work in earnes', not tryin' ter git up er great 'citement, but 'deavorin' ter show de folks de right way to live in dis worl' so da would be better prepared for de life to come; an' ef dar eber wuz er man dat wuz hones' an' true ter his callin' I b'l'ebes dat I wuz de pusson.

'Mong de members o' my flock wuz er mighty likely 'oman named Frances. I wuz fust drawed toward her by her singin', an' one time when de sweetness o' her music died away, I looked at her an' 'knowledge ter myse'f dat I loved her. At fust she sung fur my soul an' I worshiped wid her, but atter w'ile she sung ter my heart an' I worshiped her. I tried ter think o' my ole wife lying' in de shade o' de sycamo' trees, an, in my min' I could see de rail pen round her grave an' de trees would be gone an' in dar place would stan' a likely 'oman smilin' at me. I went ter my ole wife's grave an' drapped down on my knees an' prayed. De broad sycamo' leaves waved and specks o' moonlight come siftin' down like de flyin' chaff o' new oats dat ketches de light o' de fresh-born day. Er makwin' bird sung in er tree close by, but, way ober on er hill, er night hawk cried. I thought how me an' my ole wife had wucked in the fiel', side by side, an' de bird seemed ter sing sweeter, but den, twixt me an' de grave dar hung er bright smile. I tried ter rub it out wid my han', but dar it hung, an' through its brightness I seed de worm-eat head-boa'd o' de grave. "O, Lawd," I prayed, "let dis tem'tation pass herway. Let dy sarvent in his ole age hab de strenth ter turn fum de high-strung follies o' de young man." I riz up, wid de damp, dead grass clingin' ter my knees. De lights gunter shine fum de church close by, an' de sad an' swellin' song o' de congregation peared ter lay er tremblin' han' on my heart. Why did I on er sudden lean ergin er tree? Becaze I heard her voice. I went inter de church an' ez I walked wid bowed head toward de pulpit I heard somebody whisper "He's been in de woods ter pray." I did not look up but I knowed who it wuz dat whispered, for my heart felt de tech o' de tremblin' han'. I preached dat night de best I could, an' it seemed dat I made my hearers feel some o' my own sadness, fur w'en I called fur de stricken in heart ter come up ter de mou'ners' bench, mo' come forward den had eber come befo' under de 'fluence o' my callin'. We stayed late in de church dat night. Nearly all de mou'ners, habin' wuck ter do de naixt day, had dun left de house w'en I noticed one po' feller whose heart, it 'peared like, wuz almos' broke. He lay flat on de flo' an' groaned like he suffered great pain. I went ter him, raised him up an' hil' his head on my knee. De congregation thinned out, one by one. I leaned over an' talked ter de po' man. Lookin' up I seed dat Frances was kneelin' wid us.

"Lady—Sister Frances," I said, "it's time dat you wuz goin' home. De can'les is all burned away an' de lamps is goin' out."

"I will stay an' he'p you poor de ba'm on dis po' sinner," she replied.

I didn' say no mo'; but w'en mo' den er hour afterwards de sinner got up ter go, I says ter her:

"Sister Frances, if you ain't got no 'jections, I'll walk home wid you."

She smiled—de same smile dat I had seed twixt me an' de worm-eat head-boa'd o' de grave—an' said dat she would be pleased for me ter 'company her. I doan know what I said ter her ez we walked erlong, but I know dat w'en we got ter de little gate in front o' de cabin w'ar her folks libed, she wuz leanin' on my arm. De moon had gone down, an' de flutterin' in de trees in de yard told me dat de mawnin' birds wuz fixin' ter begin dar twitterin'.

"Brudder Summers," said de lady, ez I wuz erbout ter bid her good-bye, "dar 'pears ter be sunthin' on yo' mine."

"Not only on my mine, Sister Frances, but dar is sunthin' on my heart."

I was goin' ter turn erway atter dis, but she put her han' on my arm—de same tremblin' han' dat had teched my heart—an' said:

"Tell me 'bout yo' troubles. Tell me whut is lyin' on yo' heart."

"Er tremblin' han', lady."

"Does you know dat it is er han'?"

"Yas, fur I keen see it in de light o' 'er bright smile."

"Is de han' cold?"

"No, lady."

"Is it ez wa'm ez mine?" she said, ez she put her han' in my own fever-like grasp. De naixt minit my arm wuz around her. De mawnin' birds twittered in de trees, light gunter wink ercross de bottoms, an' dar, ez de gold o' de day wuz chasin' de fleetin' silver o' de dawn, I axed her ter be my wife.

CHAPTER II

We wuz married. I tuck her ter my cabin an' bright light fell on my hearth-stone. She wanted ter he'p me in my work o' 'swadin' folks ter do right. "I know," she said, "dat folks all erround us will be makin' mo' money den we is, but money doan water de flowers o' de heart, nur broaden de 'joyment dat comes ter de soul." I lubbed her deeper atter she said dat, fur I seed dat her natur wa'n't vain nur her heart set upon de flesh-pots o' de world.

Two years passed erway—two o' de happies' years o' my life. One day dar was some bills stuck up 'nouncin' dat Andrew Hennifen, er colored politician dat libbed in town, would on de naixt Friday make er speech ter de folks. Er campaign wuz on han' an' gre't intrus' wuz felt in de outcome. W'en de day come de weather wuz so showery dat da couldn' hol' de meetin' out do's, so some o' de men come ter me an' axed me ef da mout meet in de church. I didn' much think dat it wuz de right sort er meetin' ter be hel' in de house o' de Lawd, but seein' dat da wuz all so anxious, I tole em dat da mout. Den da axed me ter go ober an' lissen ter de gre't speech wut de generman wuz gwine ter make. I didn' like de idee o' settin' in my own church and lissenin' ter de skussion o' de erfairs o' de worl'. Den Frances spoke up:

"W'y, Dave," she said, "if we are gwine ter lib in de worl' we mus' take some intrus' in de erfairs o' de worl'. Ef de man had got anything wuth yearin', I doan see w'y we aughtenter go an' lissen ter him. Ef we finds dat wut he says ain't fit fer us, w'y den we ken come erway."

"Wut you says is true, Frances," I replied, "an you mus' scuse me ef I is holdin' you back in any way. Er ole man loves wid jes' es much wa'mth ez er young man does, an' it is er pity dat he doan lub wid ez much jedgment."

"You musn' talk dat way, Dave," she said, wid er laugh, "fur in lovin' me yo' jedgment ain't made no mistake."

Hennifen wuz er tall, yaller man, an' much younger den I 'spected ter fine him. In his speech he used a good deal o' strong talk, an' called er lot o' folks dat wa'n't present, liars an' thieves. I didn' like dis, but er man dat sat naixt ter me tole me dat it wuz all right, an' dat ef de speaker didn' do dater way, de folks would think dat he wuz erfeered ter 'nounce his principles. Atter de speakin' wuz over, de speaker come up ter me, hil' out his han' an' said:

"Mr. Summers, I has often hearn o' you, sah, an' I takes dis 'tunity o' shakin' han's wid you."

Wen I had shuck han's wid him, he said:

"Is dis yo' daughter wid you?"

"My wife, sah," said I.

"Ah, I's pleased ter meet de lady."

We walked on outen de house, an' Hennifen wuz so busy talkin' 'bout de gre't principles o' his party dat he didn' seem ter notice dat he wuz walkin' erway fum de crowd wid us. Atter w'ile he stopped an' said dat he reckoned he better go back.

"Won't you walk on home wid us?" my wife said.

"I thanks you kindly; I b'l'ebe I will," he answered. "I would like ter see de inside o' my 'stinguished 'quaintance's house," makin' er sideways motion wid his head at me, "an' 'sides dat, I'se got er little bizness ter talk ober wid him."

"You will see er lowly household," said I, "fur I ain't been gaged in gederin' de shinin' goods o' de yeth, but at de do' you will see er vine dat is watered wid truf an' dat blooms in contentment."

"Dar ain't no reason why dar shouldn' be some o' de shinin' goods o' de yeth in yo' house," said he. "De fack dat da is o' de yeth doan meek 'em none de less de Lawd's, an' bein' shiny doan meck 'em de property o' Satan."

I seed my wife look at him wid er quick glance, an' I knowed dat she 'proved o' wut he said. I seed mo' den dat—I seed wut until dat time had 'scaped me—I seed dat de man wuz good lookin'. I felt er pang o' oneasiness, an' I cleared my froat deep, ez ef I would rasp de pang outen my bosom. W'en we got ter de house, he set down in er rockin' cheer an' made hisse'f look freer an' easier den I had eber felt in any house 'cep' my own. Frances went inter de little shed kitchin dat j'ined de house an' cooked dinner. It struck me dat she tuk er heep o' pains, specially w'en she fotch out er table clof dat I didn' know she had. Atter dinner Mr. Hennifen said dat he would git down ter bizness.

"Mr. Summers, you is too smart er man ter be wastin' yo' substance," wuz de way he started out. I didn' say nothin'. He went on: "You hab got de 'bility ter make yo'se'f mighty useful ter yo' country. De 'fluence dat you has 'stablished ober yo' fellerman ken be turned ter rich ercount. De bes' people in dis county wants ter 'lect Hillson fur sheriff. Dis ken only be done by good men puttin' dar shoulders ter de wheel. I is Hillson's right han' man, an I's got de 'thority for sayin' dat ef you'll turn in an' make speeches fur him dat he will pay you well."

My wife looked at me. "Mr. Hennifen," said I, "wut you say may be de truf, but I is makin' speeches fur de Lawd."

"Yes, but makin' speeches for de Lawd, Mr. Summers, needn' keep you frum speakin' in fabor o' Hillson."

"Dave," said my wife, "Mr. Hennifen is sholy right, an', mo'n dat, ef dar's er man in dis neighborhood dat needs money, you is de man. De folks dat lissuns ter you preach neber seems ter know dat we needs things in dis house."

"Frances," I replied, "Mr. Hillson ain't er man o' my choice. He has been mixed up in ugly erfairs, an' I kain't make no speeches fur him; so, let de subjeck drap right whar it is."

Hennifen 'sisted on sayin' mo', but I tole him it wa'n't no use. He didn' stay long atter dis, but sayin' dat he would see me ergin, went erway.

"Does you allus 'spect ter lib in poverty?" my wife axed.

"I doan 'spect ter meck speeches in fabor o' er dishones' man," I answered.

Hennifen come back inter de neighborhood de naixt week an' called at my house, but I wa'n't at home. When I axed Frances wut he had ter say, she said dat he didn' stay but er few minits an' didn' say much o' anythin'. Er few days atterwards I hearn dat he wuz in de neighborhood ergin, workin' wid de voters, but he didn' come ter my house, an' I didn' hunt him.

Nearly er munt must hab passed w'en one day I wuz called on ter preach de funul o' er man ober in ernuder 'munity. I didn' git back till late in de night. De house wuz dark, an' ez I went up ter de do' I tangled my foot in de vine, stumbled an' tore it up by de roots. I went in an' lit de candle. Frances wa'n't dar. I called her—stepped to de do' an' called her till de echo o' my voice brought back wid it de cry o' er night bird. I went ober ter er neighbor's house. De women folks 'gun ter cry ez soon ez da seed me. I axed ef da had seen Frances.

"Oh, Brudder Summers, she's dun gone wid dat yaller raskil. He fotch er buggy an' tuck her erway."

I went down ter de sycamo' trees w'ar my ole wife wuz buried, an' got down on my knees. Dar wa'n't no bright smile 'twixt me an' de grave.

CHAPTER III

De women folks fotch flowers nearly ever' day an' put 'em in my house, an' de men folks tuck off dar hats w'en da come w'ar I wuz. I kep' on makin' speeches fur de Lawd, an' men dat wuz once noisy in church wuz now quiet.

De 'leckshun time come on, and I kotch up my old gray hoss an' rid up ter town. I went ter all de votin' places, but didn' see nobody dat I knowed. I heard one man say: "Wonder wut dat cuis-lookin' ole man is er pokin' 'roun' yere fur?" Den somebody answered: "Dar's er yaller man dodgin' 'round yere somewhar dat mout fling some light on dat question." Ever' time I hearn o' any p'litical ter-do anywhar, I rid dar, but didn' see nobody dat I knowed.

Winter time come, de col'est winter dat I eber felt. One Sunday dar come er heavy snow, an' dat night it turned so col' dat I couldn' hardly keep wa'm by de fire. De win' blowed hard. Suthin flapped ergin de winder. I hil' de candle, an' dar seed de great starin' eyes o' er night bird. I turned erway an' had jes' sot down by de fire w'en I hearn er noise at de do'; I lissened, an' den I hearn er groan. My heart felt de tech o' er col' hand, an' I knowed dat Frances had come back. I opened de do'; she lay on de groun' wid her face turned up. I tuck her in my arms an' laid her on de bed.

"Dave—Dave, won't you forgib me?"

I stood lookin' at her. "Oh, won't you forgib me? De Lawd has pardoned me, an' I has come back ter ax you—you—"

"Yas," I said, "yas, po' child. Go ter sleep in peace."

She looked at me an' tried ter smile, but de light wuz gone, an' dar wa'n't no smile 'twixt me and de grave.

We laid her under de sycamo' trees, but not w'ar my old wife wuz buried.

I kep' on goin' ter p'litical meetin's, an' some folks wondered why er ole man dat neber voted tuck such intrus' in sich erfairs.

One day I wuz ridin' 'long er road near w'ar er number o' convicts wuz at work. I seed er man dat I knowed 'cross de road in front o' me. I turned toward him. He flung up er gun and cried out:

"Stop, er I'll kill you. Been er huntin' me long ernuff."

I didn' stop, an' he fired at me, an' den, flingin' down de gun, he clim de fence an' 'gunter run ercross er fiel'. Er mighty yelpin' noise made de a'r ring, an' lookin' erway ter de right, I seed er lot er bloodhounds dat da kep' fur chasin' de convicts. Da wuz atter de man. Somebody yelled ter 'em ter stop, but da didn'. I got offen my hoss, an', wid seb'ral men, followed de dogs. We heard de man holler—we seed him tryin' ter fight off de dogs. "Mussyful God!" I hearn him cry, an' den his voice wuz swallowed up by de howlin' o' de dogs. W'en we come up ter w'ar de dogs wuz, I seed er man tore all ter pieces, an' I seed er dog, atter lookin' at me, bury his teeth in er yaller face.

Dat night ez I riz up frum my ole wife's grave, de dead, damp grass clung ter my knees.

THE CAPTAIN'S ROMANCE

Capt. Rilford is known as one of the bravest and most gallant officers of the United States army. He is one of those old bachelors to whom the passing years bring additional installments of romance. I have seen him go into ecstatic spasms over a spout spring in the mountains, and have known him to lie under a tree and shed tears over the misfortunes of a heroine drawn by some fourth-class romancer; but in action he was so fearless that his brother officers excused what they pleased to term his soft qualities.

A short time ago the captain was granted a leave of absence. He had long since grown tired of all the fashionable watering-places, and no longer could find anything in the cities to interest him, so the question of how he should spend that time, which was all his own, began to perplex him.

"I am acquainted with both the wild and civilized life of our country," said he, addressing a friend. "I know the wild Indian and the Boston swell; and, to tell you the truth, I don't know what to do."

"Yes, you are acquainted with the extremes," the friend rejoined, "but do you know much of the intermediate? You have made a study of the Indian in his wild state, but do you know anything of him as a citizen? Why not go to the Indian Territory, the Cherokee Nation, for instance, and amuse yourself by studying the habits of the Indian farmer?"

The captain was so impressed with the idea that, the next day, he set out for the Indian Territory. He found the country to be beautiful, with hills of charming contemplation and valleys of enrapturing romance. Streams like moving silver thrilled him, and birds, whom it seemed had just found new songs, made the leaves quiver with echoing music. After several days of delightful roaming, the captain rented a small cabin, and, having provided himself with a few cooking utensils, settled down to housekeeping. With the rifle and the fishing rod he provided ample food, and as he soon became acquainted with several farmers he thought, over and over again, that his romantic craving had never before approached so near to (in his own words) sublime satisfaction. His nearest neighbor, four miles distant, was an Indian farmer named Tom Patterson. His family consisted of a wife and one daughter, a rather handsome girl. She had learned to read and write, and, as she seemed to be romantic, the captain soon became much interested in her.

Patterson was rather a kind-hearted old fellow, accommodating in everything but answering questions concerning his family, but this was not an eccentricity, for nearly all Indians are disposed to say as little as possible with regard to themselves. Ansy, the girl, was fond of fishing, and as no restraint was placed upon her actions, she and the captain (his words again) had many a delightful stroll.

There was, I had forgotten to mention, another member of the Patterson household, a negro named Alf. He was as dark as the musings of a dyspeptic, but he was good-natured and obliging.

"Rather odd that a colored man, so fond of political life, should live out here away from the States, isn't it, Alf?" the captain one day asked.

"Wall, no, sah, kain't say dat it is. Dar's er right smart sprinklin' o' us genermen out yare, an' dough we's mighty fur erpart we manages ter keep up good 'sciety, sah. Yes, sah, an' ef it wa'n't fur de cullud genermen in dis yare 'munity w'y de Territory would dun been gone ter rack an' ruin. Caze why? I'll tell yo', sah. De Ingin is a mighty han' ter furnish meat, but gittin' o' de bread is a different thing. In udder words, sah, he kin kill er deer but he ain't er good han' to raise co'n. Yes, sah, de nigger ken plow all roun' de Ingin, an' de Ingin knowin' dis, ginally gins de niggah er good chance."

"You work with Mr. Patterson on shares, don't you?"

"Yes, sah; ha'f o' dis crap 'longs ter me. W'y, fo' I come yare dar wa'n't hardly nuthin' raised on dis place but weeds an' grass. I happened to meet Patterson in Fort Smif one time. He hearn me talk erbout farmin' an' den he made a dead set at me ter come home wid him."

"Are the people throughout this neighborhood very peaceable?"

"Yas, sah, lessen da gits 'spicious o' er pusson, an' den look out. Da looks cuis at ever' stranger, thinkin' dat he's spyin' 'roun' an' tryin' ter talk de Injuns in faber o' openin' up this yare territory. Dar's er passul o' fellers ober de creek dat calls darselves de Glicks. Da is allus 'spicious, an' I tells you whut's er fack, I'd ruther hab er team o' mules run ober me an' den be butted by a muley steer—an' I does think way down in my cibilization dat er muley steer ken thump harder den anything on de face o' de yeth—den ter hab dem Glicks git atter me. Seed 'em hang er pusson once jes' fur nuthin' in de worl', an' da didn' ax him no questions, nuther."

As the days passed the girl seemed to be more and more pleased with the captain. One evening they sat on the bank of a stream, fishing. The sun had sunk beyond a distant hill, but continued to pour over his light, like a golden waterfall.

"Ansy," said the captain, "this is a beautiful and romantic country; but do you not grow tired of living here all the time?"

"If we don't know any other life we do not grow tired of this one," she replied.

"You are a little philosopher," the captain exclaimed.

"I don't know what that is, Captain, but if you want me to be one I will try to be."

The captain smiled and regarded her with a look of affection.

"The great cities would delight you for a time, Ansy, and then you could come back here with a heightened appreciation of the sublime surroundings of your own home."

"The sun has blown out his candle," she said, pointing. "It is time for us to go."

CHAPTER II

The captain could not sleep. He had extinguished his lamp, but on the wall there was a bright light. It grew brighter, and then he saw that it was the face of Ansy. A rap came at the door.

"Who's there?"

"Captain, for God's sake run away. The Glicks are coming after you."

It was the voice of Ansy.

The captain dressed himself and opened the door. The girl was gone. The moon was shining. The officer was not the man to run away. He closed the door, took up a repeating rifle and opened a small window. He waited. A few moments passed and he saw several men enter the clearing in front of the cabin.

"What do you want here?" the captain shouted.

"We want you."

"What do you want with me?"

"Ask you some questions."

"You may ask questions, but don't come a step nearer."

"What did you come here for?"

"None of your business."

This reply created a commotion. The captain could hear the marauders swearing. "We'll break down the door," one of them said as he stepped forward. The next moment he had fallen to the ground. When the smoke cleared away the captain saw that the rascals were gone, but there soon came from the woods a shower of blazing arrows. It was time to get away. The captain made a hole in the roof, crawled out, sprang to the ground and hurried into the woods.

Early the next morning he went to Patterson's house. The family had heard of the fight.

"You neenter be 'larmed now, dough, sah," said Alf, the negro, "caze da foun' out dat you wuz er Newnited States ossifer, an' it skeered 'em putty nigh ter def. You gin it ter one o' 'em putty hard, I ken tell you. Shot him squar through, an' da doan think he gwine ter lib, da doan, but dat ain't no matter, fur he wuz de wust one in de bunch. Ef he dies, folks 'roun' yare will hol' er pra'r-meetin' thankin' de Lawd."

Patterson and his wife left the room, but the negro sat in the doorway.

"Ansy," said the captain, "I owe my life to you."

"Dat you does, sah," Alf replied.

The captain gave him a significant glance and again turned to the girl.

"Yes, you have saved my life, but that is not the cause of my deep—deep (he glanced at the negro)—deep regard for you."

The girl made no reply. The captain could have killed the negro. "I will ignore his black presence," the captain mused. He leaned over and took the girl's hand.

"Ansy," said the negro, "w'en dis yare generman gits through wid yo' han' I wants you ter sew er few buttons on dat ar hickory shirt o' mine."

"You scoundrel," exclaimed the captain, springing to his feet, "how dare you speak in such a manner to this young lady?"

"Why, boss," the negro replied, "what's de use'n makin' sich er great 'miration. Dat 'oman has been my wife fur putty nigh two years."

The captain's romance was ended.

OLD TILDY

In nearly every neighborhood of the South, there comes, in the fall of the year, a sort of religious wave. Men, who, during the summer swore at their horses and stopped but little short of blasphemy, in imprecatory remarks addressed to obdurate steers, turn reverently, after fodder-pulling time, to Mt. Zion, Ebeneezer, New Hope and Round Pond, to hear the enthusiastic pleadings of the circuit rider and the begging injunctions of the strolling evangelist. Robert's Cove, in East Tennessee, is a neighborhood typical of this peculiar religious condition. Last autumn, when the katydid shivered on the damp oak leaf and the raccoon cracked the shell of the pinching "crawfish," there suddenly appeared at Ebeneezer meeting-house a young man of most remarkable presence. He was handsome, tall, graceful, and with hair as bright and waving as the locks of the vision that come to *Clarence* in his awful dream. He said that his name was John Mayberry. He had come to preach the gospel in a simple, child-like way, and hoped that his hearers, for the good of their souls, would pay respectful heed to his words. A materialist would have called him a fanatic, but as there were no materialists in that neighborhood, he soon became known as a devout Christian and a powerful worker in the harvest-field of faith. He read hallowed books written by men who lived when the ungodly sword and the godly pen were at war against each other, and in his fervor his language bore a power which his rude hearers had never felt before.

One night, after a stormy time at the mourners' bench, and while women whose spirits were distressed still stood sobbing about the altar, Mayberry approached a well-known member of the church, and said:

"Who is that peculiar old woman, that wrinkled and strange-eyed dwarf who sits so near the pulpit every night?"

"We call her old Tildy," Brother Hendricks replied. "She has been a-livin' in this here neighborhood mighty nigh ever sense I kin ricolleck. She's a mighty strange old woman, but I never hearn no harm uv her."

"She may be a good woman," the preacher rejoined, "but she casts a chill over me every time I look at her. Goodbye, Brother Hendricks. Think of me to-night when you get down on your knees."

The preacher sought his temporary home. He lived about a mile from the church, in an old log cabin with one room. Many of the people had offered him a home, but, declining, he declared that he wanted to be alone at night, so that, undisturbed, he could pursue his studies or pray for inspiration.

The hour was late. The preacher had taken down "Fox's Book of Martyrs" and was looking at its thrilling illustrations, when a knock at the door startled him.

"Come in," he called.

Old Tildy stepped into the room, and, quickly closing the door, stood with her back against it. She nodded her head and smiled—a snaggle-tooth grin—and said:

"How air yer, Brother Mayberry?"

"I am very well, I thank you."

"Powerful glad ter know that folks air well."

"Thank you; but what business can you have with me at this time of night?"

"Mighty 'portant bizness, Brother Mayberry, mighty 'portant."

"Does it concern your soul?"

"Not ez much ez it do yourn, Brother Mayberry; not nigh so much ez it do yourn."

"I don't understand you!" the evangelist exclaimed.

"But I'll see that you do, Brother Mayberry. I reckon you've noticed me at church, hai'nt you?"

"Yes."

"Well, whut you reckon I went thar fur?"

"To hear the gospel, I suppose."

"Not much, Brother Mayberry; not much. I went thar to see you."

"To see me! Why on earth, madam, do you care to see me?"

"Would ruther see you on earth, Brother Mayberry, than anywhar else. I went to see you, Brother Mayberry, because I love you."

"Merciful heavens!" exclaimed the evangelist, throwing up his hands in a gesture of horror.

"Yes, Brother Mayberry, I love you, and I want you to be my husband."

"Oh, God forbid!" the disgusted preacher groaned.

"Yes, Brother Mayberry, but the Lawd hain't forbid. Let me tell you one thing: when old Tildy sets her head, w'y suthin' is goin' ter happen. Does folks cross old Tildy? Yes, sometimes. Did old Patterson cross Tildy? Yes, Patterson crossed po', old, harmless Tildy. Whut did Tildy do? She grabbed Patterson's boy an' hil him under the water till he was drounded. Did Martin cross old Tildy? Yes, Martin crossed old Tildy. What did old Tildy do? She met old Martin in the woods an' killed him, an' folks thought he killed hisse'f. Now, air you, in the bloom o' yo' youth and beauty, goin' to cross po', old, harmless Tildy?"

The cold dew of horror gathered in beads on the preacher's brow. "Madam," said he, "I cannot marry you. Your request is preposterous; your presence is appalling. Go away."

"Not until I lead my husband with me, Brother Mayberry."

"Go, I tell you, or I will throw you out of the house."

"Throw po', old, harmless Tildy out of the house? Ha, ha! Brother Mayberry!"

She took a horse-pistol from under her apron. "Buckshot in this, Brother Mayberry; ha, buckshot."

The preacher sank down on a chair. He did not care to die. In life there was such a bright promise of the good he could accomplish. He could not marry the hag, but there she stood with her awful weapon. Could he not rush upon her?

"No, you can't, Brother Mayberry," she said, lifting the pistol. She was reading his thoughts. Could he not pretend that he would marry her, and afterward make his escape?

"No, you can't, Brother Mayberry," she said. "The jestice uv the peace is waitin' outside with the license. Oh, no, Brother Mayberry, I'll not give you a chance ter run away. Wouldn't it be awful fur the people ter come here termorrer an' find Brother Mayberry with a hole through his beautiful head? Must I call the jestice uv the peace, ur shoot you?"

"Merciful heavens, what is to become of me? I cannot die this way."

"Yes you can, Brother Mayberry."

"Oh, I cannot marry this hag."

"Not this hag, but yo' own true love, Brother Mayberry. Come, whut do you say?"

The preacher dropped upon his knees. The woman advanced a few steps. The preacher heard some one at the door. Was it the justice of the peace whom the woman had under her control? A man stepped into the room.

"What does this mean?" he asked

"This horrible creature is going to kill me if I don't marry her," the preacher replied. "Are you the justice of the peace?"

The man laughed. "No, I'm no 'squire. Goin' ter kill you, eh? But what with?"

"That awful horse-pistol."

"That's no pistol. It's simply a stick. W'y this is one of her favorite games. Kill you! Why she never hurt a thing in her life."

"How about Patterson's boy?" the preacher asked.

"He's all right. I seed him this mawnin'."

"Yes, but she killed old Martin."

"Did she? I saw him not more than three hours ago. Come, Tildy, go on away."

She put the crooked stick under her apron, and, without saying a word, glided out into the darkness. The preacher lifted his hands and uttered a fervent prayer.

Note.—Riders of Monarch Bicycles say they are the very "Poetry of Motion" and a never-ending delight.